THE BLACK CITY BENEATH

Airships away!
Thanks! Rich/H2O

The Black City
Beneath

R. Overwater

Front Cover by
GMB Chomichuk

TINY SLEDGEHAMMER
CANADA

The Black City Beneath

R. Overwater — First Edition

Copyright © 2019 Rick Overwater

All rights reserved. No part of this publication may be reproduced, distributed or transmitted in any form or by any means, including photocopying, recording, or other electronic or mechanical methods, without the prior written permission of the publisher, except in the case of brief quotations embodied in critical reviews and certain other noncommercial uses permitted by copyright law. For permission requests, write to the publisher, addressed "Attention: Permissions Coordinator," at the address below.

Tiny Sledgehammer
An Imprint of The Seventh Terrace
41 Mt. Yamnuska Place SE
Calgary, Alberta, Canada, T2Z 2Z6
www.the-seventh-terrace.com

Publisher's Note: This is a work of fiction. Names, characters, places, and incidents are a product of the author's imagination. Locales and public names are sometimes used for atmospheric purposes. Any resemblance to actual people, living or dead, or to businesses, companies, events, institutions, or locales is completely coincidental.

Front Cover by GMB Chomichuk
Additional Illustration by Aaron Bilawchuk

ISBN 978-1-9992001-2-1

To Tina, John and Marie. Most days, you're the only reason I do anything at all!

Chapter 1

Wilbur peered out the front window of the Wright Cycle Company. Third Street was littered with puddles from the day's rain, but the clouds were thinning and tomorrow might well be sunny. If the side streets weren't too muddy, they could likely resume bicycle-testing the redesigned airfoils—assuming Orville and Charlie finished the latest one tonight. The sound of an argument drifted from the back of the shop. Wilbur wasn't overwhelmed with confidence.

In the dusk, he made out five or six figures in black greatcoats approaching from the end of the street. The first was a woman, a tall one, hair tied in a bun. She glanced in his direction, then to the store window beside her. The person at the rear did the same as he passed, carrying himself with the same self-importance as the government agents who'd visited the shop yesterday. Feeling strangely relieved as they faded into the street-end's shadows, Wilbur retreated to the workshop.

Orville and Charlie had calmed down somewhat. "The camber is even from one end to the other," said Charlie, looking up at Orville. He had one hand on a five-foot span of cloth-wrapped wing. "I don't think your lift formula is giving you the right numbers."

Orville stood back, combing his fingers through his hair. "You figure? I suppose Smeaton could have gotten the coefficient for air pressure wrong." He sighed. "Lord knows we've had to rethink everything else." He looked up as Wilbur entered. "Charlie thinks this next run won't do any better than the last."

Wilbur was inclined to agree, but before he could answer a loud banging came from the front door. He cracked it open just far enough to stick his head out. It was the tall woman, her entourage carefully positioned behind her.

"I'm sorry, but we are closed," said Wilbur. The door swung into his face and he stumbled back as she pushed her way in. Giving him a shove, she cleared the way for the door to open fully and a handful of men paraded in after her. The last quietly shut the door behind him and locked it.

"Into the back, Mr. Wright. Please." Her accent was thick, but hard to place. Nordic, Germanic, Wilbur couldn't tell. She gripped his shoulder and spun him about. Seeing the resolute look on the other

THE BLACK CITY BENEATH

men's faces, hands stuffed into their pockets, didn't resist.

Charlie and Orville each held one end of the wing and looked up in surprise. Wilbur stumbled as the woman shoved him toward the workbench, turning to face her as Charlie caught him.

In the light, the collars of dark green military uniforms poked from beneath the crew's thick coats. The woman was clad neck-to-toe in dark brown, rather striking. She smiled at them.

"The estimable Wright Brothers of Dayton, Ohio." Her smile widened as the three men shot bewildered looks at each other. "I have the highest respect for you two."

"What is this all about?" said Wilbur, his voice shaking.

Her smile vanished. "It is I who will ask the questions." She took the wing from Charlie's slack hands. "This is based on Lilienthal's design, no? Tell me its purpose."

One of the men dragged Charlie forward, knocking Orville aside. He twisted the older man's arm behind his back, lifting him to his toes. Charlie grimaced, but tried to look defiant. "For the front," he said. "So we don't have an accident like Lilienthal." A chuckle rippled through the men.

"An accident." The woman smirked.

3

"Those uniforms are Russian, aren't they?" Charlie said.

The woman laughed along with the men this time. "Da. Russian." Her face turned serious again. "You are Charlie Taylor, the mechanic that has been indispensable, no?"

Charlie opened his mouth as she produced a pistol. The barrel, shiny and black like polished onyx, didn't resemble anything made on a lathe. The telltale seams found in die-cast metal weren't apparent on the trigger guard, the chamber, anywhere. It had not been manufactured using any technique Wilbur was familiar with.

"I regret this," the woman said.

The pistol made a dull clack followed by a sound Wilbur would have best described as a chime—but really, it didn't sound like anything he'd ever heard. Charlie was blown backward, a perfect circle gaping at the center of his chest. Blood pooled around him as he collapsed beside the drill press.

"Charlie!" Orville shouted.

The woman waved them over to the table and chairs past the workbench. "Yes, yes. This is horrible," the woman said. "Regardless, gentlemen, I will settle for no less than every scrap of your research. Mr. John E. Wilkie himself visited you yesterday, so you know why I'm here. Please sit."

THE BLACK CITY BENEATH

A stocky man with a bent nose put his hand on Wilbur's shoulder and shoved him onto a chair. Another man did the same with Orville, while a third stood with a pistol trained on them. At the back of the workshop, a pair of men swung open the shop's large double doors as a large canvas-backed steamtruck rumbled up.

"It is clear that people like you are finally top of mind for your boorish Mr. Roosevelt. So, with the obvious exception," she waved her pistol towards the body on the floor, "We shall handle you two with a degree of subtlety."

The back of the truck erupted into a beehive of activity. Two men swept the canvas back to reveal more green-uniformed men who descended upon the workshop, unloading boxes, vertical panels on castors covered in meters and gauges, and several pieces of equipment Wilbur could not identify.

The woman nodded in satisfaction. "I am a firm believer in the old expression that dead men tell no tales."

"This is U.S. soil," Orville said. "You wouldn't get away with it."

She gave Orville a condescending smile. "Indeed, we would not. And leaving a trail of blood so soon after a visit from Roosevelt's spies would reveal that I was here. So, as I said, this is your good fortune."

R. OVERWATER

"Spies," Orville said. "There's nothing about us you couldn't look up at the patent office."

She nodded. "Perhaps not. But I'm not here because someone wants to study your noble pastime. I'm here to ensure the success of your bicycle company." She lifted the top of a wooden crate that had been placed in front of her. In it was a large black velvet bag, round in shape, cinched with a drawstring at the top. "I confess, it does my conscience good to leave a couple of people alive for a change."

She opened the top of the bag. "Although I have never truly trusted this device as much as I trust a good old-fashioned bullet." She set down her strange pistol. "Or its modern counterpart. We had limited success with Mister Tesla—let us hope things go better this time."

Four men walked up, dragging long electrical cables. She reached into the bag with both hands, hefting what first appeared to be a polished brass diving helmet. Except it had no faceplate, no intake valve for air, no apertures of any kind save for mountings that matched the cable-ends her men held. She placed it on Orville's head.

The men approached, one spinning the helmet a quarter-turn. A hollow-sounding curse emerged. They clicked the cables into place and stepped back. The woman pointed toward a man standing at a panel

THE BLACK CITY BENEATH

who threw forward a large double-knife switch. Wilbur heard the sputter of a large spark in the back of the truck. The gauge needles leapt to the right and Orville screamed.

Wilbur leapt up and reached out but someone shoved him back down. A helmet slid over his own head, smothering him in darkness and muffling the woman's voice. "Do not be afraid, Mr. Wright. It is only agonizing for a moment. Once we've begun, you will be fine."

The street was already drying in the morning sun as Bellona, the tall woman, peered through the window across from the Wright's shop. "Have we secured this storeroom for the whole day?" she asked a lieutenant.

The lieutenant consulted notes left by the previous shift. "They gave the shopkeeper a double-dose of the sickness agent," he said.

"In Russian," she snapped.

"Sorry," he said, effortlessly switching to the proper language. "They slipped it into his meal at a restaurant, so he'll probably think he has food poisoning. Bazdt has men watching to see if he feels sick enough to consult a doctor." He snickered. "Or at least what passes for a doctor up here."

7

Secretly, Bellona admired how the Hjen learned the languages of her world, their accents perfect, in mere days. Besides their scientific advancements, that was about all she admired.

"You are too far down the chain of command to be as arrogant as Bazdt," she said. "Must I shoot another one of you?"

The lieutenant grew pale beneath his dark olive skin. "Commander Bellona. I... I apologize."

"You Hjen—so smug," she said. "You think everyone will just fall to their knees when you arrive. It will be your undoing if I don't keep you in check."

"Yes, Bellona."

"Find Bazdt. Tell him I want to know why we haven't heard from our man in London yet."

The door closed behind her as she peeked through the curtain. Across the street, Wilbur was on time, keying into the lock. Orville was reported to be at the train station, picking up a shipment of bicycle gears. It was a bit of luck; she could observe the helmet's effects one man at a time. Bellona watched silently, enjoying the quiet.

Wilbur pulled the door shut behind him and she wished his building offered enough hiding places to allow her to spy from inside. Now was the test. Did the helmet work? Had they targeted his memory with a light enough touch they hadn't destroyed his mind?

THE BLACK CITY BENEATH

The answer was usually "yes" but Bellona never took it for granted. Seeing Wilbur's first few minutes at the shop would reveal much.

The thing most likely to confuse him was the emptiness of his shop, scrubbed clean of every hint of the pursuit of heavier-than-air flight. Generally their victims shrugged off any confusing details. But if her crew had been sloppy, they risked ruining the man to the point it was made public note of. Some other scientist might become interested in the Wrights' work. This was her worry with Tesla.

Nikolai was brilliant. Bellona had been fond of him in her own fashion. His visionary inventions posed as much risk to the plan as heavier-than-air machines did, so the helmet treatment was necessary. But there'd been no need to destroy the man's mind so completely.

She'd killed the Hjen engineer who botched it, and since then they'd been careful. Heavy-handed discipline didn't work on most men—it wouldn't work on the Prussians she led. You couldn't trust men in battle if they despised you. But it worked on this pig-headed lot. They were clever in many ways, but often as short-sighted as they were brutal. Their desperate need to win the coming war was no surprise.

A man, holding a little girl by the hand, entered the shop. They emerged a half hour later with a new bicycle. This was a good sign. A minute later, Wilbur poked his head out, looking up and down the street, worry on his face. Another good sign. Charlie Taylor was punctual. Wilbur would be noting that he was unusually late for work today.

Chapter 2

"Here come the big numbers, Weiss."

"Speak up." Karl Weiss cocked one ear, trying to make out the thin sound of Davidson's voice. The creaks and shudders of the bathysphere, punctuated by the occasional "SPANG", increased as it descended into the Pacific on its maiden voyage. The quartz wafer used for the radiotelephone's speaker might be less prone to moisture damage, but it didn't do any favors for the human voice.

"Seven-ninety-seven, seven-ninety-eight."

Davidson buzzed through the radiotelephone, lost in crackles of static. "Eight-oh-two, eight oh-three, eight-oh-four. Eight hundred and four feet! You are now the lowest salvage diver in the U.S. Navy."

"The new communication officer is a funny guy," Weiss said, his voice flat. "You meant *deepest*."

"You're right," Davidson sounded contrite, "Sir."

The captain's voice came on. "Weiss, the Admiral says since you're the guy setting new records today with the most advanced diving equipment Houdini

R. OVERWATER

Manufacturing has ever built, you get the honor of naming it."

"How about the U.S.S. Eaton?"

The captain took a moment to reply. "Fair enough. We all feel bad about Bill. Maybe someday you guys won't have to take these risks."

"First, you'll have to quit making dead sailors for us to bring up."

"Just fire up the lights and tell me if you can you see anything yet."

"Right." Weiss reached over to the instrument panel and flicked a switch. The inky dark outside the portholes turned blue-green. "Nothing visible yet. On second thought, wait... We're right on top of it."

With the Russian fleet docking increasingly in its Alaskan ports, the captain hadn't been surprised when a Canadian patrol ship reported a signal flare off its west coast. The watch hadn't been sure they'd seen anything at all—there was only one flare.

If there was a distressed ship, chances were good they didn't want to be found by anyone but the Russian Imperial Navy. Weiss had been sent after Russian codebooks before; this was probably another such job. It generally meant pawing through drowned Russians.

Weiss didn't particularly like testing newfangled gear, the original purpose of this expedition. He was

THE BLACK CITY BENEATH

even less impressed with testing it on a genuine military salvage mission. Still, a week ago no salvage diver could have made it this far down. There was no arguing the opportunity had to be seized.

Weiss expected another aging Karp-class sub, retrofitted to keep up with the Prussians. The Germanic naval engineers were starting to embarrass Russia's navy with advancement after advancement in response to Czarina Alexandra's Finland invasion. But what Weiss saw through the aft porthole looked nothing like a Karp.

"All halt," Weiss barked. "Hold at this depth."

"What do you see, Weiss?"

"Captain? This highly advanced machinery I'm testing? Your new bucket here might have already been one-upped." Weiss pressed up to the glass.

A long sleek shape extended out of sight, a submarine maybe, dully reflecting the bathysphere's lamps. Judging by the curvature—he couldn't see either end—it might have been three hundred feet long. Weiss didn't know of any fleet in the world with a submarine this size, nor any that could operate at this depth.

On what was probably a conning tower, a perfect circle cut through where a hatch should be. There were a few more circular breaches further down the

R. OVERWATER

hull, all about four feet in diameter. No way to tell what did this, but it had done a hell of a job.

"Can't confirm what this thing is. A sub I guess. Never seen anything like it." He grunted as he rolled his six-foot frame over to reach the gear on the bulkhead behind him. Comfort was not something this vessel was made for. In fact, this experimental bathysphere was so cramped the Navy ignored standard regulations, foregoing the rules about two-man dives. "I best suit up and take look. And captain, one more thing?"

"Yeah, Weiss?"

"Best guess is someone sunk this thing. Tell the metallurgic detection boys to keep their eyes peeled."

"Will do. But we put you down at best last-known position. It's a miracle you found it. They say the only thing they're reading down there is you."

So the navy's new metal detection equipment had its shortcomings. Weiss almost enjoyed the revelation.

"Well, what the boys can't see is quite the sight." He pulled down the roll of lifeline—two long hoses in a braided sheath and a bundle of wires wrapped in layers of tar-impregnated jute under a thick coat of Indian rubber—and plugged the lines into the hammered-brass helmet beside him. "I don't think it went down easy, and I don't want to run into whatever sunk it—the damage I'm seeing doesn't look

14

THE BLACK CITY BENEATH

like torpedoes, or depth charges, or anything you'd expect."

"You're using the atmospheric suit, correct?"

"Right." Weiss hefted the new helmet. It was very light. And the self-contained suit was a marvel for sure. For a moment, he considered trying it without the detachable lifeline. That would be a new experience. Ten years ago, he wouldn't even have dreamed it: being able to travel any direction or distance he wanted—complete mobility. That is, as long as the caustic potash solution that removed carbon dioxide lasted. He'd probably be outside too long to feel comfortable without a lifeline. Another time perhaps, in a place where he could recover from any surprises the new device might throw at him.

He'd keep the lifeline attached. Men like him—men in the field—had a tendency to throw curve balls at over-enthusiastic engineers. Often at the price of their own lives. He looked up at his lucky suit, the old Mark V he and his uncle had rebuilt. Despite the tight space, Weiss had insisted on cramming it in. It was dependable. His father had actually patented it afterward.

With only one shallow harbor dive in this new gear under his belt and now deeper than any man had ever gone, it would be nice to be inside a proven-reliable suit. But this wasn't a wreck off the Cuban coast. He'd die of hypothermia if he was in it for any extended period. He'd only brought it for peace of mind, a last-chance resort if something truly catastrophic happened.

"Putting the new suit on right now," Weiss said. It smelled like soldered brass and fresh rubber.

Exiting the bottom hatch was difficult. Odds were good the men who built the bathysphere and the engineers behind the suit hadn't consulted each other for one second. The bulky top-heavy battery on his back nearly prevented him from getting out and he swore as he wriggled into the water. He was thankful when the helmet lamp lit up.

Under the its brilliant glare, the machine below him was indeed a glossy black, not just a dark colour muted by the deep water.

"Ok, out now—toggling the ballast tank." He strained to bend the stiff elbow joint back far enough to release the small lever. Below, the sunken sub appeared nearer in the circle of light. The compressed air burbling out of the lower-back ballast tank made a racket.

His light carved through the darkness, the odd floating speck caught in its glare. Jesus, he was down deep—the furthest away from humanity he'd ever been. On any other day, he'd be enjoying this.

THE BLACK CITY BENEATH

His lead-soled boots made a small clunk as he landed on the hull. Weiss loosened one of the weights from his belt and tossed it off the side for a little more buoyancy—no telling how solid this dead boat was lying, no idea how unstable the bottom of these waters might be.

"I'm down. On the port side of this thing, headed toward the bow... I think."

"Any flag of origin?" The helmet's radiotelephone sounded tiny and faint.

"I see something. Hang on, almost there. It's painted on, looks strange on this tub." Weiss stared down at the gold outline of a two-headed eagle holding a scepter in its talons. "Right. Looks like the Russians have a few surprises docked up in Alaska."

"Roger. You said Russian, correct?"

"Yes. I'm entering the conning tower now. Big hole. No sign of a proper hatch anywhere."

Inside, the craft seemed less alien; Weiss spotted ladder rungs through the hole in the tower. He pulled down some slack for the lifeline, turned around, and slid in. The hole's sides were clean and smooth. He kneeled again and worked his way across the length of the ladder into a small cabin.

He could see what looked like a bridge, judging by the seating, towards the bow. A couple of bodies lay on the cabin wall, splayed haphazardly the way only

17

R. OVERWATER

true corpses can manage. There were a lot more empty chairs than bodies. Two books hung chained from what was probably the navigation desk, if the map etched on a large metal daguerreotype plate was any indicator. The map wasn't of any landmass Weiss recognized. He reached into his pouch for his steel cutter, snipped the chains, and stuffed the books into a leg pocket.

Working his way over the lights and protuberances from the bulkhead he stood on, he made it to one of the bodies, kneeled, and rolled the man over. There was a perfectly circular hole in his chest, similar to the holes in the hull. Every navy in the world recognized the men's long-sleeved shirts, the black and white striped *telnyashka*. "Couple bodies here. Russian for sure. Funny, just these two guys."

In the distance to his left, he saw a movement. Lights blazed in his eyes and then a black boot-sole kicked into his faceplate. His head clanged against the helmet-back and he fought to stay on his feet, his light illuminating them from the side. Weiss swore.

"What's happening, Weiss?"

Two black suits stood before him, hard and shiny looking, the furthest one aiming a rifle that appeared to be of the same material as the sub and the suits.

18

THE BLACK CITY BENEATH

Before he could answer the captain, the second man bounded forward and rammed the rifle butt against his head, jerking Weiss' neck and sending him crashing down on the bulkhead.

Everything was flashes and shadows, random blows and confusion, Weiss fighting to orient himself. He reached for a deck chair, bolted to what should have been the floor, and began to pull himself up. The rifleman fired his weapon and the deck chair on his left vanished in a boiling swirl of grit.

"Weiss!" The captain crackled in his ear.

The two men turned toward each other, one leaning forward and nodding. Weiss' heart pounded like a mallet. Then they turned and sprang away, a blast of bubbles propelling them into the dark.

"Son of a—"

"What the hell is happening down there? Can you report?"

"Just met some of the crew. Left as fast as they came. I may have taken some damage to the suit." He let go of the chair and brushed by another as he tried to make his way forward. Something on his back shifted and everything went black.

Weiss froze, lest he stumble or entangle himself before he figured out what was wrong. Scraping through the bathysphere hatch probably damaged the lifeline and loosened the emergency battery. Reaching

19

all the way behind him was like bending one's arm in a stovepipe: he couldn't do it. But he could tell everything was out of position.

"Captain?"

"Ahoy McKinley."

Nothing. And nothing he could do about it. Not without taking the suit off. He'd done that before. Unlike then, he was in frigid water right now, dark as night and almost three times deeper than he'd ever been. He wrapped the lifeline around his left arm and began pulling it tight with his right.

He inched forward, following the line and laying the slack off to his side. Hopefully it would spool up without snagging back at the 'sphere—but who cared about the Navy's new toys? He'd be happy if he just made it back.

The ladder in the conning tower was a spectacular obstacle. It couldn't have been harder to contend with if it had been vertical. His heavy feet kept hooking in the rungs. When he tripped, he smashed his knee in the chink where the suit-leg was articulated for walking. Sweat trickled down his forehead, stinging his eyes in the blackness. Grunting as he wrested himself upright, he was stricken with light-headedness and fell back down on one knee. Right. Of course.

THE BLACK CITY BENEATH

The lifeline wasn't delivering air. He was overtaxing the air scrubber—assuming it was still getting battery power—and depleting the tiny supplemental air tank. He had minutes to get to the bathysphere before his air ran out, and his decision-making would be less reliable with every second. The cold was seeping in through the suit's skin. The battery-powered heater must have conked out as well.

He could make out the dimmest of light on the other side of the tower's breach. He climbed out, crouching to avoid losing his balance and falling off the hull. That would do him in for sure. The faint glow of the bathysphere was a welcome sight.

He unfastened micro-weights on either side of his belt until he felt sufficiently buoyant. Standing up gingerly, he kicked the lifeline slack off to one side so his legs didn't tangle. Gripping the taut line with both hands, he leapt up towards the light.

Shivering uncontrollably now, his dizziness from the lousy air barely tolerable, he gave the lifeline a few tugs. It was enough to bring him up into the floodlights under the bathysphere. The blurry outline of the open hatch took shape. One hard pull and he was there, thrusting his head and shoulders into the hole, but he couldn't get any further. He was stuck.

What little space he had getting out must have been lost when everything on his back got knocked off-kilter. He kicked his feet with all his waning strength to no avail, and fought the urge to panic. He relaxed, slowed his breathing, and thought for a few seconds.

He reached behind him to the ballast tank and purged the remaining air. The pull on his legs was instantaneous.

Weiss had spent plenty of time underwater with his father and uncle, determining how to best get a man out of seemingly inescapable situations. Hopefully the engineers had gotten their take on his father's first patent—the separating collar that allowed a diver to remove the top of a compromised suit—correct the first time. He thumbed the relief valve on his helmet, so that the combination of depth pressure and negative helmet pressure wouldn't mash him into paste as the sea attempted to push his entire body up into the helmet. He'd seen the gruesome effects of "the squeeze" once and doubted there was any worse way to die. Feeling the valve rotate into place, he reached down and triggered the release collar.

It worked. Tiny explosive charges made muffled "poks" and the stabbing cold of 800-feet-deep seawater shot through his body as he wriggled and kicked until the suit-bottom slipped away. Pressure assaulted him from all sides.

THE BLACK CITY BENEATH

Gripping the remaining suit's bottom, he pushed hard to get down beneath it, the full force of the ocean squeezing him like a vice. Already his limbs felt like spaghetti, but he wedged his face past the jammed suit into the air. One breath, as much as the pressure on his ribcage would allow, and he summoned enough strength to squirm in up to his chest. This was as far as he could make it.

He had to make it. And soon, or he wasn't going to, ever. What would his father or uncle have done? They were escape artists, entertainers, not deep-water divers. There was nothing in their training that prepared him for this.

He looked around for anything that would help. The winch that spooled out the lifeline was just in reach. Wrapping one arm through the lifeline from the reel side, he groped for the return lever, snagging it with his fingertips. The winch clanked into gear, the motor whirring as it tightened the line.

It nearly wrenched his arm from its socket. He tensed with what little strength he had left, feeling his thighs scrape as the line dragged him between the suit and the hatch frame. When he got his knees over, he reached to the winch and switched it off, falling to one side and panting. It took a couple of minutes to notice the blaring radiotelephone.

23

R. OVERWATER

"Master Diver Weiss, respond. This is the USS McKinley. Master Diver Weiss, can you respond?"

"I'm here."

"Are you all right? Can you report?"

"Had a small problem with the suit. And the hatch is jammed. Gonna lie here for a little while and then I'll fix it."

"Are you fit enough to do the prescribed decompression time?"

"Yes sir."

"We'll debrief you later then. See you in eight days."

"Right." Weiss breathed slowly, feeling his head clear, warmth seeping into his bones, wondering why he was still alive.

Those guys down below could have finished him. For some reason they didn't.

Chapter 3

Rainy Washington State. John Mulholland lifted his flask in mock salute to the grey sky outside the cabin window. *Rainy, cloudy, goddamned miserable-cold Washington State.* This was no place for a Kentucky boy.

In a couple of weeks when the last substation was finished, for whatever-the-hell the army needed so much electricity for, he could go home and spend some time on the Ohio River. He'd stick a jar of Old Man Saunter's three-county bourbon under the skiff's seat, forget he was Deputy Chief Engineer, and forget how chilly the northwest coast was.

A knock rattled the cabin door. He stoppered the bourbon flask and jammed it in a desk drawer.

Corporal Nash stepped in. A knowing grin spread across his face as he watched the drawer close. "At least the civilians are staying warm while we wait for more coal."

Mulholland smiled back. "That's exactly why I keep it here." He waved the memorandum he'd been reading, more stamps and seals than actual text. "What the hell is Big Bertha getting me into this time?"

Nash winced at the insubordination. Major Bertha Tharp was not actually big, but as Chief of Engineers in the U.S Army Corp of Engineers, she carried herself that way. The engineering corps was one of Roosevelt's jewels, and anyone who didn't respect or fear her simply didn't know better.

Mulholland continued, undeterred. "Why am I flying to England with a navy salvage diver of all people? I've never heard of this Weiss guy. Isn't it a big enough pain in the neck that I've got to run the biggest electrical project ever attempted, and they're keeping me in the dark about it?

Nash shrugged. "Don't shoot the messenger, Chief."

Mulholland chuckled. He had to do something about his habit of thinking out loud. With Nash it wasn't an issue, but it would get him into trouble one day. "Guess I'll know soon enough. It can't be any worse than this job." He stood, motioning Nash towards the door. "I take it the new process engineer is here?"

Nash stepped out onto the wooden milk crate serving as the cabin's step. "He's over at Substation C."

THE BLACK CITY BENEATH

The Substation C building, far more solid than anything the army put its staff in, was only half above ground. Nash held the door for Mulholland and they ducked as they entered the low doorway and descended the steps. Two privates knelt in the blue glow of a meter bank at the end of the room, removing various items from a small crate and laying them in a neat row.

A slim man in his late twenties, nattily dressed, rose and extended his hand toward Mulholland. He was probably another civilian, seconded from his role at some big company, same as Mulholland. "Mr. Mulholland, Alex Smith. Pleased to—"

Mulholland frowned as he spotted the man's wedding ring. "What the hell is that on your hand?"

Nash cleared his throat. "Forgot to mention, we got another newly-dead in the ranks."

The new man's smile faded. "Newly dead?"

Mulholland spread his arms wide, looking around. "See all this open wiring, switches, busses, and *that*?" He pointed at a massive block of porcelain, pierced by a steel bolt thick as a hickory stump. It had an eyelet on either end, foot-thick cables snaking out in every direction. Smith nodded.

"We're running this whole base on about 100 megawatts right now, and that's just nominal voltage while we wait for Major Tharp to fly in and oversee the main generator installation. Then we're jumping voltage up to 250 kilovolts, all running through this base from three different lines. Any metal out of place in here—like that ring—might cause a spark to jump and fry something real good. No unnecessary metal in here, period."

He held up a tanned hand, a white band where his ring had been last week when he, Nash and the two privates were chasing steelhead in the Little Hoquiam. "You best wear the fisherman's ring while you're on site—'less you want to go back to your new bride as a shoebox full of cinders."

Nash grinned, holding up tanned hand with a similar band of pale skin. So did the two enlisted men over by the meters. One of them spoke up. "Corporal, does this means I'm off the oars finally?"

"You bet." Nash turned to Smith. "Fishing with the Deputy Chief is mandatory. New guy always rows. As much as the Chief grumbles about the weather, we've been getting sunny days on the river."

Smith stiffened. "I've never fished in my life. I'm here for the work. What would you have me do, Deputy Chief?"

"Call me John. You and I aren't in the damned army." He led the engineer and Nash past two voltage converters, their giant copper coils sheathed in

THE BLACK CITY BENEATH

hardened paraffin. "Corporal Nash will explain everything but, before I leave you two, any questions?"

"A couple. I understand we're in this particular bay because we need shelter from the weather, while still using minimal line to reach the shore."

"But...?"

"But you hired me on as a process engineer to oversee efficiency. Why do we have generators and substations spread over five miles inland? You've got four times as much transmission line, not to mention redundant lines you're backing them up with. And there's increased fuel expenditures for inter-site travel, extra communications infrastructure. Why isn't it all centralized? The extra time and money wasted is astronomical."

"Well, tell me, Smith. What's easier to bomb? One site, or several?"

"This is a strategic military site?"

"That's exactly what I asked when I was railroaded into this job." Mulholland tried to feign a grin. "Can't say they really gave me an answer." He looked at his watch. "Speaking of no answer—don't know why I'm being sent to England at 1700 for a meeting with a bunch of stuffed suits, but I am. Corporal Nash, you're in charge."

29

R. OVERWATER

The army possessed the fastest dirigibles this side of the Atlantic, so the fact Mulholland was flying on a civilian luxury blimp instead was a pleasant surprise. The Army captain assigned to see him off didn't seem as pleased.

The captain was in civilian clothes and looked awkward. "There's an attaché case in your cabin." the captain said. "Combination is your wife's birthday plus the..." He looked at a slip of paper concealed in his palm. "...square root of a hypotenuse as counted from the third mark on a protractor." He tore the scrap up, put half in his pants pocket and let the rest casually slip from his fingers.

Mulholland squinted for a moment. "Got it."

"Really?"

"The goddamned army didn't talk me into leaving Westinghouse to be its second highest engineer for nothing."

"The Navy guy is on board. Meet him in the bar at 1800."

"How will I know him?"

"Easy. Watch for a big strong guy who looks pissed off."

The Astraeus wasn't called the "Titanic of the Sky" for nothing. Ever since the Titanic established Atlantic dominance, routinely setting new records, every passenger company in the world compared its

THE BLACK CITY BENEATH

flagship craft to the massive ocean liner. The Astraeus had earned it. Half as much duralumin frame as the average dirigible, three times the resistance to lateral torsion—the English built damn good airships.

A porter took his bag and Mulholland walked up the gangplank. He drank in his first sight of the interior framework, sprawling above like a giant steel web, knitted together with thousands of feet of gangplanks and affixed passenger cabins. They could get a lot of folk into these things now that the gas cells were smaller and more evenly distributed. Calculating the right ballast must be a pain; you couldn't simply jettison passengers when a drastic altitude change was required, and the right amount of water needed to be in the ballast tanks when they took off.

Mulholland tipped the porter before twisting the ornate handle on his cabin door. The attaché case the captain mentioned sat just inside the doorway. Dropping his luggage, he picked it up. The leather was cool to the touch and the lock on the case's stiff over-flap, elegant in its plain design, was a Houdini. The army didn't use anything but, and they came with any number of tricks—such as seizing after one failed try. He took a moment to make sure he had the combination right.

Chapter 4

After a week in a tiny decompression bell, the Astraeus' lounge seemed cavernous. This was a fine place to enjoy a drink and Weiss certainly deserved one. Unlike the men in his crews, he abstained as often as not—he took his responsibilities seriously, too seriously if you asked his men—but not tonight. He had two down already and no plan of stopping.

He could have used a couple drinks back in the decompression bell. Day after day, the little quartz speaker buzzed with questions from a stream of Naval officers. The same questions, over and over. It became clear the Russian Navy had been caught in Canadian waters more than once, and it was also obvious someone had recently seen strange submarines near the Juan De Fuca Strait.

They, on the other hand, dodged every question he asked about the submarine, and when they announced his next assignment, they were elusive about that too. It itched at him more and more as he lay there, licking his wounds.

R. OVERWATER

He'd never been in a fight underwater before, never mind one hundred and thirty fathoms down. It angered Weiss the Navy might have known what they were getting him into, but there was no better place to be than out at sea, far away from everything and everyone. Not only did joining the Navy give him that luxury, it let him play at the top of his game, and that meant accepting what he'd signed up for and keeping his head down. He'd had a good run, more peaceful days than not. Hopefully his lucky streak wasn't over.

His glass was empty and he looked up to order another one. At the edge of his peripheral vision, a man approached, staring at him. Weiss swiveled in his chair and met his gaze.

The man stopped in his tracks, looking unsure. His paunch suggested plenty of time at a desk. His moustache needed grooming and his suit was well-worn, but he had the look of a person used to being in charge.

Weiss pulled the card he'd been given out of his pocket. "Deputy Chief Engineer Mulholland?"

"John is fine. Master Diver Karl Weiss, right?

"Right."

"Can I buy you a bourbon?"

Weiss pulled out the chair beside him. "Another whiskey would be swell."

34

THE BLACK CITY BENEATH

Mulholland sat and called the bartender over. "Two bourbon, no ice in mine."

Weiss saw the pasty white of Mulholland's neck as he extended it, contrasting a face and hands almost as tanned as his. On the back of one wrist, a small cut was healing poorly.

Mulholland caught Weiss staring at it. "The army teaches men a lot of things," he said. "How to properly cast with a rod and reel is not one of them." He grinned. "But guess which guy had to clean all the fish?"

Weiss could tell the man was waiting for a reaction. The engineer was a talker. Fine. An evening of conversation it would be.

"I didn't know engineers actually went outside into the real world," said Weiss.

"Well, I suppose we're full of all sorts of surprises."

Weiss let the silence hang.

Mulholland pressed on. "You'd think Washington would be crowing about it the world over, but I heard from Major Tharpe you set a new bathysphere record. Safe and sound below 800 feet. A lot of pressure down there. I'd love to see the blueprints. The boys who built it must know what they're doing."

Weiss smacked another empty glass down. The bartender whisked it away. Mulholland gestured for another.

"Tell that to Bill Eaton." A fresh drink slid in front of Weiss and he took a sip. "He was supposed to hold the record and be basking in the glory right now." He took a sizeable gulp this time. "They decided to keep him down for seventy-two hours. But the first bucket had a two-ply hull and they didn't account temperature differential between the two hulls and how that affects metal. The rivets on the outer hull shrank in the cold and let seawater in against the inner membrane. Some slide-rule jockey never imagined it having to perform at anything less than room temperature." He pointed at the bartender and crooked his finger.

The bartender looked at Mulholland. He nodded and the bartender set another drink down for each of them.

Weiss had pushed Eaton out of his head when he learned he'd be piloting the second attempt. He hadn't realized until now how angry the whole catastrophe made him. Topsiders—they guessed on paper about machines no one had ever built, to use in places they'd never been to.

"So the inner hull shrank even worse, and separated from the outer hull, allowing more water in.

THE BLACK CITY BENEATH

Then a seam popped on the inside. A seam on the outside followed right after. It was even odds whether the pressure would crush him or if he would drown." He swirled the ice in his glass. "It was a bit of both. He managed to get his helmet on, but the air line was crimped shut, and he was pinned by bent steel all around. I made a point of staying below deck when they cut his body out."

"Who built it?"

"*Levasseur Ouvrages Maritimes*. In Paris."

"They build the second one?"

"No."

"Well? Who did?"

"The Houdini Manufacturing Company, personally overseen by the magnificent man himself."

Mulholland motioned for another drink. Weiss might be knocking them back on this particular evening, but it wasn't a regular occurrence. He could tell it was a practiced habit for the engineer.

"Well there you go," said Mulholland. "Houdini is a marvel. I took my wife, Althea, to see his great Questionorium in Chicago. There's this one machine, it looks like an orchestra made of clocks combined with a player piano, all burnished copper and polished brass, every part machined to a thousandth of an inch. Able to call forth all the great works of

37

R. OVERWATER

Man. His people really know how to put something together."

"They do. But men who build great things often dismantle other things in the process."

Mulholland downed his drink and glanced up at the bartender, who immediately brought two more. Weiss finished the one in his hand and exchanged it. He could feel the warmth of the whiskey creeping up.

Mulholland extended his hand. "Look. It feels like we're getting off on the wrong foot here. We didn't even shake hands, and they're pairing us for a job that comes all the way down from Roosevelt. I've got that from the head army engineer herself."

Weiss gave him a cursory handshake. Not getting along wouldn't get him back to sea any quicker. "Fair enough. Was there a satchel in your cabin? You need to—"

"Mister Weiss? Mister Mulholland?"

Weiss and Mulholland swung around to find an immaculately groomed, uniformed man addressing them. The colored bars on his white jacket, the gold epaulets—he had to be captain of the Astraeus.

The woman beside the Captain was something else. Her short blond hair ended in tight curls against a long, exquisite neck adorned with a gold chain, terminated by a single black pearl. Almost as tall as he was, her svelte figure was draped neckline to toe in

38

THE BLACK CITY BENEATH

a fitted green velvet dress that no soft, spoiled socialite Weiss had ever known would fit. She was lean, hardened even, for someone who enjoyed privilege.

"Captain Stanley Tipton at your service." The captain shook hands with both men. "My lovely guest here is the Countess Iris DeHavilland."

She flashed a wide smile. "Good evening, gentlemen." She didn't look like an Iris, Weiss thought. She was English, but had the air of old-world Europe about her. A European nanny probably raised her while her parents pursued their idle, wealthy lives.

Mulholland rose from his chair. "Pleasure to be in the company of both of you." He elbowed Weiss. "I'm John Mulholland."

Weiss stood. "Karl." It came out quietly.

"Well, sirs." The captain caught the bartender's eye, pointed at the men's drinks and tapped his chest. "Consider yourselves my guests. I'm told Mr. Mulholland in particular might enjoy a tour on the bridge of the finest airship ever built. Please join us." He took Miss DeHavilland's arm, and they turned to exit. The lady casually disengaged her arm and adjusted her dress. She glanced over her shoulder.

Mulholland leaned into Weiss and elbowed him for the second time, reeking of whiskey. Weiss likely

39

smelled of liquor too. The meeting felt awkward.
Probably because he was rarely drunk.

Chapter 5

Mulholland would have been content to stay at the bar, even if it meant drinking with the Navy guy, but later he would have regretted missing the chance to see the heart of an aeronautical marvel. He summoned his best courtesy, asking about the layout of the Astraeus and its vital workstations as they made their way to the bridge through the ship's corridors.

The bridge's lighting was kept low for better visibility into the darkness outside, and it hummed with activity, punctured by unobtrusive bells and buzzers. Attentive crewmen busied themselves at their workstations, faces lit from below by the glow of their consoles. "Captain Tipton on deck," somebody shouted. The captain put four fingers to his hat brim without looking at anyone in particular. A bell rang with three sharp clangs. "We're approaching the next station," a voice called out. Mulholland looked down. The voice came from a hexagonal glass pit at the rear of the bridge, where crewmen manned telescopes on a scaffold surrounding its rim.

"We're approaching an Atlantic stationary balloon, part of the air travel corridor's signal chain," the captain explained. He swept his hand back like an opera conductor. "Redundant telephone lines to the engine room, a lookout solarium with six men on telescopes, and a twenty-four-hour four-man signal team." Beside Mulholland, signalmen flashed their shuttered lights at the balloon, sending status updates and passenger messages to be flashed forward to other balloons until they reached a telegraph station in England.

No one noticed how close Miss DeHavilland had strayed to the bank of signal lights. She bumped one, causing a random flash. "Oh!" She put one hand to her mouth. "I suppose I should be more careful."

Mulholland suppressed a chuckle, watching the captain try to stifle his reaction. Weiss was trying not to smirk too. It was doubtful the captain would react so calmly if it was one of them interfering with a critical instrument.

The tour went on for several minutes. Weiss asked questions that made him look smarter than Mulholland would had given him credit for. Mulholland's eye was drawn to Lady DeHavilland. He wasn't the only one. The crewmen did their best to be

42

THE BLACK CITY BENEATH

inconspicuous, stealing glances at her as she walked about the bridge, smiling and getting closer to their stations than they should probably allow.

In his previous career at Westinghouse before his secondment to the Navy, Mulholland had unveiled several great inventions to the upper crust. It was an occupational annoyance at this stage of his career. The ladies tended to nod demurely, giggle perhaps, and were often-as-not bored stiff. The way the countess looked around, it reminded him of a cooper's hawk, sleek and clever, barely noticeable up above, its perfect vision catching every detail.

"Oh, call me Iris, *please*," she said to Mulholland as they found their way back into the gentlemen's club. Captain Tipton escorted them to a table and pulled a chair out for her. She paid him no attention. As she leaned forward, the pearl-like globe on her necklace dangled away from her neck.

The pearl resembled the small, black cube in the case awaiting Mulholland when he'd arrived on board. He'd tried scoring it with his penknife, but it refused to be scratched, whatever it was made of. He had yet to read the information accompanying it; he'd needed to go meet Weiss.

"I have something similar to your beautiful necklace," he said, reaching into his pocket.

R. OVERWATER

"Oh, do let me see," she said, sliding her hand across the table as Mulholland set the cube down.

Weiss's hand came down on top of hers. "I'm afraid he's forgotten the rules about army property," said Weiss. "I have to look out for this guy. Wouldn't want him getting into hot water."

Mulholland struggled to say something to quell the awkwardness, but fortunately the lady was unfazed.

"Well," she said, pulling her hand from beneath Weiss' rough paw while touching it with her other, "then you *must* tell me of your recent adventures at sea. I won't take no for an answer."

Weiss slid the cube back to Mulholland. "Not much to tell. The Navy sinks something, maybe someone dies, I go down and fix it. Or bring it back up."

"Oh, don't be so humble," she said, leaning in. "Ordinary men don't acquire those muscles. Or those scars."

A waiter appeared with a bottle of wine; the captain must have called for one unnoticed. "My compliments," Captain Tipton said as the waiter poured three glasses. "It's been my pleasure. If you are interested in joining me in my morning rounds, I'll be leaving the bridge at 10:00 hours. Good night."

THE BLACK CITY BENEATH

The Lady DeHavilland murmured a response, barely looking up. Weiss touched his forehead in a faux salute. The captain stood there stiffly for a second, then walked away.

Mulholland sipped the wine, white and too sweet for his tastes, listening to Miss Iris pepper Weiss with questions. She rarely broke her gaze, looking into the big man's eyes with a smile that could melt butter. It was more than Mulholland could take. It was getting late. He finished his glass and followed the good captain's example.

Mulholland kept his eyes shut when he woke. His mouth tasted like burlap and it took a moment to place the background noise of the Astraeus.

He retraced the previous night's events, pleased that he could remember it all. Rarely needing to record a number or read a project's schematics twice, it was a bad sign if there were memory gaps after a night out. It had been a problem when he was younger, but as he rose in his profession, moderation, or more accurately, good judgment on when it was all right *not* to be moderate, had become his watchword.

His family, four generations of temperance-minded military men, blamed the bottle when Mulholland tried to enlist and was deemed inadmissible. And here he was, working for the army,

45

the right man for the job. Since he wouldn't see combat, his brothers would probably heap scorn on him anyways.

He stayed beneath the covers, making sense of last night. Weiss was a wet blanket if he'd ever met one, and the captain and Miss DeHavilland's intrusion had been welcome. He had no idea why the brass was pairing him and Weiss, but he hoped it was over quickly.

Consciousness crashing over him in waves, Mulholland swung his legs to the floor and reached for his toiletry kit. He pulled out a packet of headache powder. The attaché case still sat by his luggage. He stuffed it beneath the bed. What was Weiss going to tell him about it before they were interrupted? Something to talk about over breakfast.

He locked the door and headed for the stairway leading to the restaurant. Even the airship's stairwells were elegant, all burnished oak and brass handrails.

A waiter was pouring Weiss a second cup of coffee as Mulholland approached. Mulholland flashed a grin and Weiss looked up. "Yeah?"

"Well." Mulholland signalled the waiter as he sat. "You know I have to ask."

Weiss sipped his coffee. The man actually looked rested on five hours of sleep. "Ladies like that are out of a seaman's league."

THE BLACK CITY BENEATH

No surprise. Weiss didn't strike Mulholland as a ladies' man. "Hell," he said. "Even in my prime, a gal like that wouldn't have given me the time of day."

"No matter," said Weiss. "Can't say I liked her. Too nosy. I had to tell her a hundred times the questions she was asking could get me sent to the brig."

Weiss paused as the waiter arrived, staying silent until Mulholland ordered breakfast. It was several minutes before he spoke again. "And that reminds me, you dumb—" Weiss closed his mouth and looked away for a second. "When you showed her that black cube from your attaché case—" He stopped, seeing Mulholland's expression.

Mulholland bit his tongue. That exchange had definitely rankled him, but he felt too rough to get into an argument about it. Breakfast arrived and he dug in, relinquishing the chance to answer.

"Take this from a guy who's seen sailors get robbed on every continent," Weiss resumed. "We need to keep our mouths shut. They put us together for a good reason. We have a job to do and I don't think we're going to like it." Weiss dropped to a near-whisper. "I've seen that black stuff before. The biggest damn submarine I've ever seen is made out of it and *that's* lying on the bottom, a half day south of the Juan de Fuca Strait." He pointed at the cuts still

47

healing on his face. "There's plenty of people more interested than her in my so-called adventures. And they're a lot less charming."

Mulholland sat upright. Weiss would have been diving in his neck of the woods. "The biggest electrical engineering project ever is happening near there." He lowered his voice. "A diver and an engineer. Why would they pair two guys like us?"

Weiss looked over at a busboy clearing a table. "I don't know. But maybe you're the paper pusher that finally gets me killed."

Mulholland's face grew hot.

Drawing a slow breath, Weiss put one palm on the table. "Look. I'm the best at what I do," he said. "And supposedly you are too. If you keep your eye on the ball, I'm not hard to get along with. Now, what I was supposed to tell you last night is to cut out the lining of that case that was waiting for you. There's a bunch of engineering plans to read up on. I'm guessing it leads to whatever I've got to do."

Mulholland speared a piece of sausage with his fork. "My wife will give me no peace at all if she learns I'm doing something dangerous. Good thing soldiers will be handling any rough stuff."

"Right." Weiss folded his arms. "Dangerous is the only kind of work I do. And now you're working with me."

THE BLACK CITY BENEATH

Mulholland felt ill as he unlocked his door. He gazed wistfully at the bed before noticing the attaché case. It was out from under the bed. Opening it confirmed his fear; the lining was torn out and nothing remained inside.

He darted into the hall and ran up the stairs. Weiss was on the next tier up and he wasn't sure where else to go. He skidded to a halt at Weiss' door. There was a circular hole where the lock should have been. As he pushed into the room a thick forearm engulfed his throat, choking him mid-breath and pulling him backward. He was flipped to one side and his face hit the floor.

The grip relaxed almost instantly. It was Weiss. Jesus he was strong. A hand extended down. Mulholland grabbed it and Weiss pulled him to his feet. Mulholland rubbed his jaw.

"Sorry." Weiss swung the door closed and pulled Mulholland off to the side. "Whoever put that hole in the door is still on board and you don't want to be in front of the thing that made it. Guess they couldn't jimmy the lock after I jammed it."

"Jammed it? But the locks are Houdinis," Mulholland said. "They're supposed to be the most secure locks in the world. Mine was beaten somehow and whatever was in my case is gone."

49

"You just have to know the right tricks," Weiss said. He pulled a wad of folded papers from his back trouser pocket. "Look. They've got your mission. But they don't have our destination."

Mulholland arrived at a satisfactory plan first. "We've got to find the captain and see if he can flash a message to the mainland."

Weiss nodded.

Mulholland pulled out his pocket watch. "He did say he'd be on the bridge if we wanted to join him on his morning rounds." It had seemed more of an invitation to the lovely Miss DeHavilland, but he'd take it.

Two burly men with sidearms blocked their entrance as they approached the bridge. One pushed his chest against Weiss, thwarting his efforts to bluster through. "There's been a weapon discharged and two break-ins," Weiss said. "We need to speak with the captain right away."

A man with black curls sticking from beneath his cap appeared behind the guards. "I'm Acting Captain Garret," he said. "This is the bridge of a world-class airship. What is your business here?"

"Where's Captain Tipton?" Mulholland asked, trying to seem composed. "He invited us here last night and we—" The acting captain looked at the guardsmen, who drew their pistols. The acting

THE BLACK CITY BENEATH

captain wheeled his finger in the air, and the guards marched the two into the bridge, positioning them against the aft wall.

"Now then." The acting captain stared straight into Mulholland's eyes, shifting his glare to Weiss next. "You gents were with Captain Tipton before he was murdered in his quarters."

Murdered. Mulholland caught his breath.

"There was a lady on his arm when he found us," Weiss said. "She might have seen something that can help you."

"If you mean the Countess DeHavilland, she is missing and we are concerned. Four members of the Russian consulate are also unaccounted for, as is the captain's log book and, until now, you."

A guard spoke up. "This one." He jabbed a finger at Weiss. "He reports weapons fired and a break in, maybe same as the countess' room."

"I bet there's a hole in the captain that matches the one in my door." Weiss said.

The acting captain was quiet for a moment. "Holster your pistols, men," he said. He beckoned Mulholland and Weiss toward his chair, limping slightly.

"I know military men when I see them," he said, easing into his seat. "I was in the Navy myself. Now I'm embroiled in a matter falling into the closest

51

constabulary's jurisdiction. They are 7,000 feet below, 300 miles away, and it will be nightfall before we reach London." He looked into their eyes. "If you gentlemen have the foggiest idea what is happening here, I suggest you inform me."

"I'll tell you what I know," said Weiss. "We are assigned to rendezvous with a roomful of brass at Scotland Yard. We haven't been told why. And if the countess' room was broken into too, whoever did it might think she —"

A trail of jagged holes spattered along the gondola glass and the airship pitched to one side.

Garret leaped to his feet and pushed aside two pilots slumped dead over the controls. He straightened the yoke and pulled a mouthpiece from the console. "This is acting Captain Garret. All passengers prepare for emergency disembarkment. Repeat, all passengers prepare for emergency disembarkment. All staff, action stations level two." He flipped open a hinged, glass bubble and toggled a switch, starting a cacophony of alarms. Whirling about-face, he shouted, "Why haven't I got a magnetometer report?"

The men at the magnetic detection table were dead in their chairs, and one guardsmen was attending to the other. Weiss was flat on his stomach, looking up at Mulholland. "Get down!" he shouted.

THE BLACK CITY BENEATH

A grey dirigible floated into view, blocking the blue expanse of the Atlantic below. A side gunner was shouting over one shoulder from his turret. Mulholland dropped down on all fours. Another seam of bullet holes stitched its way across the bulkhead, running down the console, prompting sparks, voluminous black smoke and the acrid smell of burnt wiring.

"We're losing ballast! I have to get to the emergency control gondola!" Garret shouted. Another hail of bullets peppered the gondola and he fell to his knees, a dark spot distinct on the white uniform above his chest insignia. Behind the captain, the rest of the crew lay dead too.

Mulholland seized Weiss by the arm and jerked him to his feet. "Come on!" Weiss looked doubtful, but he followed. They darted into a stairwell, down towards the axial catwalk running the airship's length.

"We need to get to the backup gondola under the tail," Mulholland shouted above the alarms. "If it isn't shot to hell. We have to stop draining ballast, maybe vent some gas, and shut the engines down before we're frozen and dead at the edge of the atmosphere."

The catwalk was clear and there were little staff to be seen. Mulholland didn't know what "action station

R. OVERWATER

2" was but this was a passenger vessel bearing hundreds of souls so it was likely crash preparation.

They ran beneath a klaxon, so loud it was painful. The deck hatch to the control gondola appeared and Mulholland stopped, gripping the railing that encircled it. His breath came in deep, burning gasps. This was far as he'd run in quite some time.

Weiss should have been right behind him, but the man was sixty feet back, against the catwalk railing, one hand to his ear, wiggling his jaw. He saw Mulholland and made his way up to the hatch as Mulholland spun it open.

Slipping, practically falling down the ladder, Mulholland searched for anything resembling a valve control. He spied a series of switches and knobs under an etched metal plate: "Ballast." It stood to reason that the venting was uncontrolled, a result of gunfire striking the tanks, and pumping the remaining amount of fluid into an undamaged tank was the only hope. He seized a knob named "tank transfer valve" and twisted it. There was a small clanking sound and he flicked a switch marked "pump," hearing the rush of fluid in pipes overhead.

His heart sank when he saw the altimeter. No wonder his breath was short. They'd shot up three thousand feet since the attack began. It was getting

THE BLACK CITY BENEATH

colder too. But that wasn't the problem; rather than level off, the altimeter was dropping now.

Not only was a ballast tank punctured, clearly gas storage had been hit too. One had merely been leaking faster than the other. Mulholland wasn't sure if all the gas compartments were connected, where a leak might be or how it could be stopped. He couldn't see any options among the limited controls of the emergency gondola, and trying to solve the problem back on the destroyed bridge would be a doomed man's quest. The Astraeus was going to crash.

Weiss stood at the ladder's bottom, face racked with pain. He looked unsteady on his feet. There was no time to ask why. Outside the fore window, people filled a row of tiny pods dotting the ship's underbelly. In the aft-most pod, close enough Mulholland could see panic on his face, a uniformed man waved at them.

The radiotelephone bank undoubtedly connected the two pods, but he couldn't make out any number on the pod ahead that corresponded with the array beside him. Mulholland did know that to escape safely, the pods needed to be out, away from under the Astraeus, so he scanned the control banks, grateful he wasn't on the bridge. There wasn't a machine built he couldn't figure out, but the sparely outfitted emergency console made it easier. He located the deployment switches for the pods. Electric motors whirred into service as he flicked them.

A dozen rails swung out to the sides and the passenger escape pods slid down, dropping off the ends and surging upwards as their gasbags inflated. They trailed in rows on either side as the Astraeus passed them.

The eight engine throttles were directly in front of him and Mulholland pulled them back in alternate pairs to keep the ship straight. They'd lost another 500 feet but the sky was clear and he could just make out the English coast.

Airspeed was down to 35 knots—about 40 miles per hour. He did a quick calculation on rate of descent, hoping the Astreus would come down in the countryside past the coast. It was better than crashing at sea, but Mulholland doubted it would be a smooth landing. He didn't want be on board to find out.

Not seeing any apparent switches for the backup pod, he looked up, spying two pairs of red gondola-release handles numbered one through four. Weiss, pale, sweating profusely, already had one hand on the first and was looking straight at him. "Go!" Mulholland yelled.

The veins in Weiss' forearm bulged and the scraping sound of reluctant metal cut through the

THE BLACK CITY BENEATH

din. He grunted as he pulled down the next two. Mulholland stepped over to Weiss, adding his full weight to the remaining lever. His stomach made a sickening leap as the gondola detached and plummeted downward.

Nobody was in control of the airship now and it was agonizing to think there might be souls still trapped aboard the rudderless behemoth. The pod jerked momentarily as it reached the end of the deployment tether and the rush of compressed gas drowned out the roar of the wind. A balloon billowed into shape above the skylight.

Mulholland was finally able to slow his thoughts and take stock. Weiss was slumped in the corner, panting. His skin was blotchy. "Were you shot?" Mulholland asked.

Weiss shook his head. "The bends. I'm only one day out of a decompression chamber." He pushed himself up on one knee, grimacing. "I doubt any diver ever went so far above sea level this soon after a dive."

Mulholland looked at the altimeter and airspeed gauges. They were still carrying some speed and landfall looked like a possibility. Below, Astraeus, still under power, plowed into the water. He imagined the physics at play, crumpling it and rendering it flaccid, trapping any survivor who might float up beneath it.

57

They overtook the doomed airship and it disappeared behind them.

Chapter 6

The doctor tossed a folded copy of the London Times onto the cot beside Weiss. "You're lucky this is simply a mild spell and we can handle the pressure differential."

Weiss sat up and took the newspaper, trying to hide his disorientation. Once he recognized the metallic tang of the voices outside, he realized he was in a bathysphere.

Right. The Royal Navy search team had detailed four men, arriving almost immediately after Mulholland set them down, to take Weiss to the deck of the HMS Haldane and get him into the first pressurized vessel they could find.

His right ear was ringing. He could make out some sound through it, but it was not as clear as his left.

"You should be free to meet your partner for a pint by mid-afternoon," said the doctor. He smiled. "You were fortunate we were taking this girl out tomorrow and the deck crew had her ready be

R. OVERWATER

dropped. As a naval physician, I'm embarrassed to realize how obvious it is that the extra drop in pressure must be accounted for if a diver is going to fly afterwards." He shrugged. "All these scientific advances. They create new problems that catch you by surprise."

"Right." Weiss flopped back down, unfolding the paper to expose the full headline: *Astraeus shot down over Atlantic. Russia denies involvement.*

He hadn't seen any Russian markings on the attacking airship, but apparently a few had. Surprisingly, nearly all the passengers survived. The crewman who had signaled the emergency control gondola to release the life boats was being hailed as a hero.

On the inside there was a smaller story: *Russian delegates missing, presumed deceased.*

Before finding that strange submarine on the ocean floor, Weiss had never given two thoughts to Russia. His father was Austro-Hungarian and family stories were the extent of what he knew about that part of Europe. The port at Copenhagen was the closest he'd ever been. Now suddenly, Russians seemed to be everywhere.

The airlock hatch squealed a couple of hours later. The next sounds were Mulholland's voice and that of an Englishman. "We're here to pick up Master

60

THE BLACK CITY BENEATH

Diver Weiss of the USS McKinley," the English voice said.

"And tell us if he's been talking your ear off," Mulholland said. "If he has, he's probably suffered a head injury that will require further care."

A new steamcar, all chrome and mirror-black finish, awaited the trio just off the dock. Weiss looked back at the open water stretching out to the horizon. He envied the sailors shipping out tomorrow. Leaving the world behind was always better than having it leave you. Once he stepped into that steamcar, there would be no freedom for a while.

He stumbled as he stepped up to the sleek steamcar. His ear rang loud as hell and his balance was definitely off. It was long odds whether he'd be fit for active duty again. Something best kept to himself.

The grey-haired British man, wearing a morning coat and matching suit that would cost Weiss a month's salary, opened the door and ushered the two Americans into the spacious back. He climbed into the seat across from them and pulled the door shut. "William Melville," he said, extending his hand to Weiss. "Mr. Mulholland filled me in regarding your recent trials."

Weiss recognized him from a photograph in his father's office.

R. OVERWATER

For a moment, the roar of the steamcar's boiler was the only sound. Then Melville cleared his throat. "Well. I won't mince words gentlemen." He paused and closed the window between them and the driving compartment.

"You two are at the center of no small amount of controversy. Some feel Mr. Mullholand here has genuinely cocked things up by letting sensitive information slip away. Others feel the blame should rest on the shoulders of those who would trust a Yankee salvage diver and a civilian engineer to handle such a delicate task. Those shoulders being mine, Max Wilkie of the U.S. Secret Service, and Major Tharpe, whose permission we needed to pair you two up. We—"

"Hold on," said Weiss. "In the past two weeks I've been shot at by Russians under the sea and Russians above the sea. You need to tell us what's going on, and why it's us in the first place."

Melville was unruffled. "We have a decidedly sticky piece of work that requires the hands-on skills of two such as yourselves. If Mr. Mulholland refuses, as is his right, we are truly up against it. And you can't be replaced by just any diver but, fortunately for us, your protests won't mean much to your superiors."

THE BLACK CITY BENEATH

Melville opened a finely carved teak panel and pulled out a decanter of scotch and two crystal tumblers. He filled each a quarter full and passed them around. Weiss could tell it was all Mulholland could do to keep from snatching it from his hand. Who couldn't stand a drink after yesterday? It tasted of warmth and peat, and could be well followed by a few more and then a hot bath and a mattress with clean sheets.

Melville poured one for himself and took a sip. "We have gotten off to a bad start. Let me apologize. You gentleman have been through a barrow-full as of recent, and neither of you signed up for the duties of policemen or soldiers. Nor do you have that kind of training." He gestured to the window. "Take a look outside."

A clean cobblestone ribbon stretched out behind them, framed by market shops, metal-smiths, and the gas-lamps waiting to illuminate the nighttime of modern London. "This is not the England of Dickens stories," said Melville. "The civilized world is changing beyond imagination."

The car rounded a corner and a large red brick building complemented with ornate white stone appeared in the distance. "Let us forget for a moment that Russia, despite a personal communiqué from Tsarina Alexandra to her Majesty denying it, is behind an unprecedented attack on civilians over English waters. We are closer than ever to a war on a global scale."

Melville sipped his scotch before speaking. "If you divulge what I am going to disclose today, you will be charged in an American court of law. And *you*," he looked at Weiss, "You will be court-martialed. I have all that on good authority from your superiors."

He pointed toward a group of blue-clad workers stepping off a tram, newspaper boys and chip vendors pushing up to capture their attention. "They think the world we know is still largely as it was five, ten, twenty years ago. In reality, everything we know about our place in the heavens has been shaken."

The car pulled up in front of a tailor's shop. "First thing, her Majesty appreciates the loss of property and hardship you've endured in her service. The least we can do is fit you for new... duds. That's what you'd call them in Kentucky, no, Mr. Mulholland?"

"Sure," said Mulholland. He brightened. "I'm wearing the only things I own right now."

In back of the shop, a balding man with a mouthful of pins kneeled by Weiss and stretched a measuring tape down the inside of the diver's leg. The tailor seemed oblivious to everything around him, lost in the motions of a daily routine.

THE BLACK CITY BENEATH

"There is a Russian spy, Bellona, and she is an unbelievably slippery character," said Melville. He pulled up a chair off to one side of the fitting area. "She has been spotted on American, British, and Prussian soil with Russian operatives. If our new allies in Prussia hadn't discovered her base here in London, she'd likely have cooked our goose within a fortnight."

He looked at the tailor, who grabbed his list of measurements and ducked behind a curtain. Melville leaned in. "Her purpose seems to be twofold." He looked at Weiss. "You're no doubt familiar with Nikolai Tesla. He's in a sanatorium now after being found outside of his flat, the door kicked in. There's a similar tale involving two brothers in Ohio. Our aeronautical chaps say they were on the brink of something big but the brothers claim no memory of it whatsoever, despite a trail of letters and purchase receipts indicating otherwise."

"Well," Mulholland cut in. "Tesla is brilliant, but I met him at the St. Louis World Fair in 1904. He's..." He raised his eyebrows and tapped one finger on his temple.

"It's more than that," said Melville. "This woman possesses a devilish device that renders brilliant minds no more capable of scientific innovation than

R. OVERWATER

your average chimney sweep. And that's not what's truly troubling."

The tailor emerged with two suits. "Apologies, sirs," he said. "We will have your new clothes sent over in the morning. I hope these will suffice for the evening. Our compliments."

Weiss took his without saying anything. Mulholland laughed out loud. "Off-the-rack suits from an expensive London tailor—they might be good enough for a Kentucky farm boy and a navy man."

That evening, as the maître d' waved attendants in and around the posh restaurant table at the hotel they'd been put up in, Weiss had to admit the suit felt good. Sure, he wished he were back at sea, but it wouldn't be so easy going back to noisy salvage ships, unforgiving bunks, and bland meals in a mess hall. As his wine glass was filled, and filled again, and the succulent food slid down his gullet, his thoughts returned to the same place. This could have been his life.

He absorbed the atmosphere, the clink of cutlery, and the smell of a chef-managed kitchen, conversations filled with idle contentment. Even at age fifteen, it had seemed natural to separate himself from these pampered, pasty people—the insufferably

THE BLACK CITY BENEATH

self-important wealthy and the leaders they influenced.

As far as the world knew, Weiss' parents had no children and they'd maintained that illusion perfectly. Uncle Hardeen, left to care for him when his father all but disappeared to do the bidding of the elite, was much less famous than his brother. Hardeen secretly resented the need to curry rich society's favor for the sake of his entertainment career and that made sense to Weiss. He remembered his uncle, on quiet afternoons, trying to teach Weiss more than just the family tradecraft; how to negotiate this world of wealth and excess while masking one's contempt.

"Those people influence everything they touch, for good or ill," Uncle Hardeen said one afternoon as they sat at a table, studying the mechanisms of a dismantled padlock. "Smile, be polite, take what you need from them and don't let them know what you really think. Never say more than you have to."

Then they murdered his uncle, those who would reshape society no matter the cost to other people. The only solution was to flee it all. Until now, that plan had worked.

By obligating himself to the Navy, Weiss had managed to limit the ability rich people had to interfere with his life. If they could interfere, they at least had to do it by influencing the Navy and they needed to be especially powerful to do so. For the most part, he had found the escape he needed. Down below, deep in the ocean, in a world these people here could never imagine, making life and death decisions every day, the work he did mattered. Weiss himself mattered. And the sea, all its mysteries and the exotic places it carried him to, what was not to love about that?

Weiss lived dangerously, but it was known danger a strong man with his wits about him could handle. This world was different. This was a world even the Navy answered to. A world where the petty maneuvers of millionaires and politicians were paid for with the blood of young men they wouldn't lower themselves to shake hands with on the street. Here, staying fit and planning ahead, maintaining the equipment your life depended on—all the things that kept him alive so far—couldn't save him from being stabbed in the back.

He was a weapon, someone else's weapon, in a war with no rules. If he'd stayed put as his uncle and father both wanted, learned to entertain these people, he'd be one of them now. He'd have a woman like the Countess DeHavilland on his arm and be more or less assured of still being alive in two weeks, two years, two decades.

THE BLACK CITY BENEATH

"Let me see if I have your story straight," said Mulholland, who'd been stuffing his face eagerly. He laid his fork down, the lines on his forehead becoming prominent. "A Russian woman erasing the memories of our most brilliant inventors. A portal in the ocean almost a mile down, another entire world collaborating with Russia—and together they plan to invade the U.S. It's like something out of a Jules Verne novel."

"You forgot one player," Weiss said, turning to Melville. "This bit about the Prussians. Everyone just can't wait to lie in the same bunk together, can they?"

"Our biggest source of embarrassment," said Melville. "That someone could be operating under our own noses—well, there are some who practice the arts of misdirection and deception at a truly higher level," he said, looking at Weiss. "You, of all people, would most certainly know."

Mulholland shot Weiss a puzzled look.

Melville set his cutlery carefully on his emptied plate. "Queen Victoria was notified by the Kaiser himself the day before our gents raided a suspected anarchist flat they'd been keeping an eye on. A messy bit, really. A Prussian operative was killed trying to get into Scotland Yard to slip us a warning while maintaining his cover. Our boys simply didn't know.

69

For whatever reason, the Prussians are keeping better track of Russian activities than we are."

Weiss pushed his own plate forward, thankful the waiter was there to pour a coffee. All this talking, hours of it, and no end in sight. His ear still rang and he was short on sleep.

"Our world was shaken when we saw that flat," said Melville. "We obtained the machine they used to destroy memory and we have only the foggiest on how it works. How the Prussians captured so much evidence is a bit of a mystery, but sealed in one wall, everything was there; notes on how to use it, how to forge that black material, details on a society whose technology eclipses ours and, most importantly, their plans to use U.S. soil as the beachhead for an invasion."

Another world. His mind reeled, but this wasn't the time to be shocked, he could ponder it later. "That sub I found," he said. "If its armaments are as advanced as the rest of it, a fleet of them might be unstoppable."

"Yes, and to make matters worse, the Russian fleet will be on their side. It's a finely wrought conspiracy that would look like the work of the Kaiser instead of the Russians—if the Kaiser hadn't reached out to us," Melville said. "It's by the grace of God we know as much as we do."

THE BLACK CITY BENEATH

Melville folded his arms, leaning back. "The rest can wait for tomorrow's briefings." He waved the maître d' in. "Marcel here has the most excellent humidor in all of London."

The maître d' bowed his head appreciatively. "Mr. Mulholland, if you could assist him in selecting three fine cigars for us, I would have a word with Mr. Weiss."

Mulholland and the maître d' threaded their way through the tables, many of them now empty as guests filed their way toward the coatroom or smoking room. Melville leaned in, his voice dropping low. "I didn't want you to learn of this tomorrow. It's been everything we can do to keep it out of the papers."

Melville looked from side to side, barely moving his head. "Your father has been one of our trusted confidants and sources of information—and innovation—since he first came here for his engagement at the Alhambra Theatre. It was at my advice that he left the stage and better applied his brilliance to manufacturing. Not only has he developed a great many things for society, he has secretly created devices of great use to your country and allies like us. *And* it has been a perfect distraction from his primary occupation—using his skills for subterfuge and espionage. You will likely

71

R. OVERWATER

never know of some of the perils your father has saved us from."

Weiss had always known his father was up to more than he would admit to. This was the first time it had been spelled out so clearly. "So you're the man to blame," he said. "Well, he always did care about a big show more than he did his own family."

Melville looked taken aback. "Your efforts to eschew your legacy have been blatant. The U.S. Secret Service, myself, Scotland Yard and MI5, we've respected that until now. You might not know, I was with your uncle the night the anarchists bombed his performance."

A waiter came, presented a piece of paper, and spoke into Melville's ear.

"Hardeen Houdini was my friend every bit as much as your father," Melville continued. He frowned. "Though he was categorically against some of your father's decisions. At any rate, right now, the newspapers believe your father is missing—presumed dead like your uncle. We've forbidden them from publishing that. We hope he is simply out of contact for a good reason. But if he is indeed dead, I know for a fact that his estate is bequeathed to you. Someone will eventually learn you are the only living heir to the great Harry Houdini. You will have absolutely no peace, ever again."

72

THE BLACK CITY BENEATH

"I'm hardly getting any peace as is," said Weiss.

Melville's look was a mix of pity and brutal pragmatism. "And now the life you chose to spite your father has landed you smack in the middle of his business. I wish it were someone other than you that stumbled into the submarine but, then again, I can think of no more suitable man for this particular madness."

Weiss didn't respond. His eye had caught a stocky, preoccupied-looking man retrieving two coats and walking into the foyer. A tall, sinuous woman in a tight, elegant dress, her back turned to the restaurant, reached out and took his arm.

Weiss had recently been in the company of a lady similar in appearance, who carried herself exactly the same way.

Chapter 7

Mulholland took a deep breath of the cool air permeating his hotel room balcony, set a sheaf of papers on the chair beside the door, and unwrapped the half-finished cigar he'd saved from dinner. Below him, a pair of lamplighters worked their way up the street. Someday they'd be obsolete because of men like him.

The gas lamps threw shifting pools of luminescence onto the limousine tops as they circled in and out from under the hotel awning. A horse-drawn carriage, gleaming with polished, exquisitely detailed wood and shiny metal fittings clattered up and a very old, rich-looking couple emerged. High above, airship lights blinked in the darkness as they traced their way across the London skyline. The Brits hadn't wasted any time turning sea power over into air power. It was enough to sting an American engineer's pride.

The occasional smack of horseshoes did little to lift his spirits. He'd sold his horses when he'd accepted secondment into the army engineers—their care would just be too much work for Althea by herself. All this—he looked out at the glimmering expanse of London, the bridge lights glowing above almost everything else—made his Kentucky acreage seem even further away.

Before dinner, he'd sent word to Althea, assuring her everything was fine but that he might be out of touch for an extended period of time, and to discount anything she might read in the papers. He hoped that statement alone wouldn't get her all worried.

He drew a match along the balcony's stone edge and huffed the cigar back to life. It was the finest cigar he'd ever smoked, and the fact he'd extinguished it and retreated from the smoking lounge was a statement unto itself. Accepting everything he learned today had proved to be difficult. He'd instructed the maître d' to advise his cohorts that he was retiring for the evening.

Mulholland turned on the balcony lamp and picked up the papers. He shuffled past the pages of text and concentrated on the schematics. So this was the machine they were building. The one that, if it worked, would devour all the electricity Mulholland could produce. Hopefully Nash wasn't hitting any snags back in the states.

THE BLACK CITY BENEATH

He followed the flow of power twice, giving careful scrutiny to the field radiators they'd deploy near the ocean floor. After Weiss anchored tethers for future equipment, Mulholland would have to follow him down with a full crew in a second bathysphere. He read the whole package twice, hoping he didn't really need to be on hand. But there were too many things that could go wrong, unforeseen problems that would need workarounds from an engineer in the field.

Mulholland was past fifty and slowly going to seed. In no way had he signed up for this. Years ago, he'd agreed to use his experience for his country. Deep down, he did it just to try live up to the Mulholland legacy of national service. The plan was to do that from the safety of his desk, on a workday that ended in time for dinner.

If he and Weiss did get into a scrape, maybe he'd earn one of the medals that eluded his brothers. Probably, he'd just get killed.

Pressing his thumb down, he scrubbed away the match scuff he'd left on the balcony's polished limestone. Below, Weiss emerged on the arm of what appeared to be the Lady DeHavilland. She'd made it out of the Astraeus crash safe and sound it would seem.

Weiss had taken a few beatings lately. The guy deserved the company of a distinguished lady.

Mulholland slept better than expected and was ready when William Melville knocked on his door at seven a.m. Melville was blunt. "Your counterpart will not be joining us," he said. "As important as our morning tour is. I had the front desk ring for him and they claim a woman answered, saying he is indisposed."

Mulholland laughed. "Well done, Mr. Weiss." He grabbed a large envelope off the hotel room desk. "If need be, I'll brief him once we complete the afternoon presentation."

"I'm not U.S. Navy," Melville said. "It's not like I can order him otherwise."

Melville summoned a steamcar and within the hour they were in the brick-lined laboratories beneath Scotland Yard. The tour was heady stuff and it was good to have Big Bertha along. Barely over five feet tall and sharp as a blade at sixty-plus years, it was hard to say what was more impressive: her to-the-bone questions for Melville's scientists, or how much she already intuitively understood.

"Mr. Wilkie will have his own questions and information to impart when he arrives," said Major Tharpe. She looked over at Mulholland. "He'd be here but his airship was secretly rerouted for obvious reasons." Her voice was thin with a tinge of rasp, the

THE BLACK CITY BENEATH

only thing besides her greying hair that bespoke her age.

Everything Mulholland examined raised more questions than answers. The mysterious helmet the Prussian spy had unearthed, purportedly used by the Russians to wipe select memories of noted scientists, made some degree of sense. Mulholland knew the human brain bristled with electrical impulses; that a device could interfere with those was not implausible.

He rolled it over in his hands, nearly fumbling it once much to the consternation of the lead scientist who rushed in to catch it. "With all due respect," the white-coated gentlemen muttered quietly, "We've been working on this project for months and repellent field generation is *our* discovery. Handing it over to a butter-fingered Yankee is a bit of an insult." Mulholland would have felt the same way if it were him.

Some of the helmet's surface connections made sense, with leads that seemed to be for positive and negative charges, and ground wires. Some had a fourth lead connected to all three—in essence a short circuit. That was odd. Others were paired, some apparently both negative on one side of the helmet, some positive on the other side. Melville's scientists surmised that the head or brain itself completed these partial circuits. The fundamentals of all this otherworldly technology, the way electricity was harnessed, challenged everything he thought he knew.

There was considerable power generated by the smallest of sources. He marveled as a scientist raised a pistol, with the same dark carapace as the sample he'd been given, and fired it. There was no recoil. Only a small chiming sound and a perfect hole in the four-inch thick cast iron target-plate gave any evidence it was being deployed. He felt the hole's smooth edges. The destruction seemed to occur at the atomic level— *seemed* to, no one really knew. And they proposed to somehow reproduce this and use it to fight the society that had invented it.

Melville's men had cobbled together an alloy of known metals and the strange black substance, hammering their alloy into a wire and heavily insulating it. When a current passed through, the amperage emerging from one end was greater than at the source. Mulholland peeled back the insulation of the test wire after Melville's men passed the charge through it. It looked slightly depleted.

Electricity. The flow of electrons, Mulholland thought. "Is something happening to the mass when a charge passes through? Something that increases the amount of electrons as the current flows? Some sort

THE BLACK CITY BENEATH

of change at the atomic level?" By the time he realized he was thinking out loud, it was too late.

A few of the scientists gave him blank stares. "That's just one question," Mulholland continued. "The Washington shoreline has retreated a few feet over the past year. I'll bet it's the same all around the Pacific and I'd hazard a guess it's because the ocean of this other world exerts less pressure. Our ocean might be slowly draining into theirs through the portal. If it is, the sea will keep flowing through it until the pressure equalizes."

All eyes were on him now. "If the drainage is high enough, this could be as catastrophic as any war. Shipyards and docks could be miles inland, international trade and travel could be crippled. Are we sure we're not going to make things worse when we deploy your repellent field generator?"

The pride in Major Tharpe's expression was almost chilling. She clearly had faith in him to practically apply these experimental forays and repel an invasion. A full-scale attack by a technologically superior foe. There would be no second chance.

Having unlocked the secrets of the pistol, their best idea was to turn it into an even bigger weapon, one that could vaporize an enemy fleet as it came through the portal or be modified to simply "push" like an invisible wall. The work of Melville's team was

81

admirable, but it struck him as shortsighted. What if the device didn't prevent the Hjen from making it to the surface? Even if it did, what about the long-term effect the portal itself was creating? Surely Mulholland could come up with a better idea.

The briefing was in a brightly lit room and Mulholland stuck out among the men and women in military uniforms. Melville and Wilkie were the only two other men not in uniform, commanding figures nonetheless as they took turns at the podium.

"This is one of the gravest violations of United States sovereignty and security we have ever witnessed," said Wilkie. "The simultaneous stamping out of scientific intellect, combined with the actions of Russia of late, leave little doubt; this is about more than a strike at American soil. These two collaborators plan to dominate the entire civilized world."

Wilkie stepped back and Melville approached. "We agree with my colleague that the evidence against Russia is overwhelming," said Melville. "As such, we are prepared to retaliate as soon as they lift a finger." He paused. "But we cannot see why Russia would proceed in this fashion."

He shuffled his papers. "Russia would lose if they did not have a superior force backing them. One has

THE BLACK CITY BENEATH

to wonder why such a powerful enemy would concede any control at all to the Tsarina once they are here. Regardless, we are fortunate Kaiser Wilhelm chose to share information about this enemy, the Hjen. A less worldly leader would try to manipulate things to his own advantage."

Major Tharpe was up next, her delivery even more terse. "Many of you," she tilted her head toward a mixed row of officers from the King's Royal Rifles, "have already received a full tactical military briefing this morning, and my job is to make sure that Mr. Mulholland can do *his* job. So I'll summarize things as briefly as possible from the Army Corps of Engineers' perspective."

Mulholland fidgeted in his chair, only half listening. He'd been neck deep in the defense project's construction for two months now. He would prefer to have been aware of that before yesterday. Nonetheless, he had a pretty good handle on what he was doing back on the Washington coast.

Melville was in the back, talking quietly with Wilkie and two men in U.S. Navy uniforms. About the absence of Weiss, no doubt.

They all glanced toward Mulholland. He could feel the uniformed men's eyes locking on him.

83

Chapter 8

Bellona scanned the London sidewalks through the steamlorry's windscreen, watching for carefully nonchalant eyes that might be tracking them. "Can I trust you to know your way?" she asked.

The Hjen driver, looking uncomfortable in his stolen, ill-fitting steampilot uniform, nodded. Bellona swiveled and pulled the curtain back to see if Weiss was conscious yet. Slumped forward, he lay on bench with a thick hood over his head.

"He's still out," said Bazdt. "You must have hit him pretty hard. Did you do it before? Or after?"

"I specifically told you I want a man watching his hands," she said. She pointed at the smaller of the two soldiers sitting alongside Bazdt. "Do as I say."

Bazdt shrugged. "He's not getting away."

"He might surprise you."

"What makes this one so damned—" Bazdt was interrupted as the lorry swayed, making a sharp left turn. The soldiers braced themselves against the steam lorry panels.

R. OVERWATER

"We're in the warehouse alley, Madam Bellona," said the driver up front.

Bellona stepped into the back and pulled a Russian-issue revolver, an old Nagant with a scratched barrel, from a small sack on the floor.

"Where are you going with that primitive thing?" asked Bazdt. "Take one of ours."

"Do not concern yourself," said Bellona. "I will be fifteen minutes. If there is trouble, don't fight. Allow yourself to be arrested and go quietly."

Anger clouded Bazdt's face. Bellona didn't wait for him to protest, putting her face close to his. "Must I establish who is in charge? In front of your men?"

Bazdt snarled, wrapping one hand around Bellona's throat. "It is only out of loyalty to my Supreme that I tolerate you. You are a fighter, but in my hands, you wouldn't last—" His eyes shifted down to the pistol pressed into his belly.

"Do you really believe you would live long enough to get into a fight with me?" Bellona spoke crisply. "I will be back soon. Follow orders and you will all be on your way home tonight."

The lorry was parked by the correct entrance. She opened the door and stepped into the shadows.

Grunvald and two younger *Schattenpistolen* waited in a small, drab office on the warehouse's top floor. Fear was all over on the younger men's faces.

THE BLACK CITY BENEATH

They were waiting to give her news. The senior man spoke in Russian as soon as she pulled the door tight. "Melville got everything."

Bellona was silent. The Supreme would be unhappy to learn their secret cache was compromised. "Oberstrasse?' she asked.

"Dead. He attempted to infiltrate Scotland Yard as ordered, but they caught him."

Well, one less to worry about. "What do they know?"

Grunvald brightened. "We were warned they were going to raid the flat. So the Kaiser contacted the queen and told her we had evidence of a Russian spy and that our man had already disposed of him." He smiled. "Then the Kaiser berated her for killing Oberstrasse when he was simply trying to inform them without being compromised."

"You spoke to the tailor and the waiter?" Bellona asked.

Grunvald nodded. "They heard enough to be convinced the English and the Americans both believe it. So that is good." He stroked his beard, looking uncomfortable again. "But, the invasion plan. They think the Russians are behind it, but they know considerably more than we thought."

"We already knew why the Americans stationed Mr. Mulholland on the west coast," said Bellona. "Now we just have to be more wary."

A junior Prussian spoke up. "It is good then that the army engineer is dead."

"He and Karl Weiss not only survived, they are in London." Bellona let the shock register. "Weiss is not going to be problem, but they are briefing Mr. Mulholland today."

"But you've seen the Hjen science. He's no match for it, correct?" Grunvald asked.

"John Mulholland is not a stupid man," said Bellona. "Whatever he is working on, it will be a hindrance."

"What do you want us to do, Bellona?" the other junior man asked.

"A word with you alone, please, *Gospodin* Grunvald." He followed her into the adjoining room and closed the door, looking mildly puzzled.

"Let us speak German," she said. That way, she'd hear the arrogance so evident whenever he spoke his native tongue. "Tell me again of your first days as a captain in the *Landwehr*."

He swelled slightly. "I was decorated for capturing the first Austro-Hungarian towns when we established the new border."

"What became of the civilians?"

THE BLACK CITY BENEATH

His tone became stern and matter-of-fact. "It was war. Those towns were rife with sedition."

"Let us return to the men."

Bellona motioned for Grunvald to go first and followed him through the door. Her pistol barked as she put a shot into the back of his head. The other men leapt to their feet as he fell. They dropped in quick succession as she fired off two more rounds.

She had forgotten how vulgar a pistol sounded in a small room. Hjen weapons didn't make so much noise. Ejected shell casings lay by the wall. She toed one to the middle of the floor.

The engineer was supposed to be dead. Melville knew more than she'd liked, though she hadn't counted on him staying in the dark forever. Everyone was still chasing the Russians; that would have to be good enough. She'd tied up the loose ends in London as best she could. She'd have Weiss, the lost prize, in the Black City by tomorrow. The Supreme would have all the American spies he needed to maintain control after the invasion. That would be enough to abate any anger over losing their secret materials in London.

She pulled out her watch. Twenty minutes. Bazdt would maintain his post but would be getting nervous. Grunvald lay on his face in a puddle of blood just inside the door. Carefully, she stepped over him.

R. OVERWATER

It was too early to be satisfied. She felt it nonetheless. Her list of men to kill was still long, but now there were fewer Prussians on it.

Chapter 9

The hood was hot, stifling, itchy, and Weiss took a deep breath as soon as they pulled it off. He blinked, his eyes reluctant to adjust to the light. Coarse, steady vibrations rumbled through the vehicle—they were moving, most likely on a cobblestone London street.

High, grey panel walls framed the double door at the lorry's rear. He could tell by the roar beneath the road noise that the boiler was beneath them instead of up front. Not a military transport then. Most likely, some sort of delivery lorry.

His hands were tied behind him. He shook his head, fighting off disorientation made even worse by his still-ringing ear. That was nothing compared to the throbbing in his skull, emanating from the tender spot where they'd hit him.

It was no small thing to knock a man out without severely injuring or killing him. Whoever hit him was practiced at it. His eyes ceased swimming and he began to make out surrounding figures. Two men sat on the bench across from him, small, shiny black pistols aimed at his chest. A stocky man with a bent nose leaned into view. The man from the restaurant.

He peered into Weiss' eyes. "He's coming out of it," the man said. "She hit him pretty hard but he'll be okay."

The man's hair was thick and wiry, black like the other men's, but obviously dyed. Orange roots sprouted from his scalp. His squat skull seemed made to weather a beating, and his nose hooked to the left, an obvious lump on the bridge where it had been broken.

The man sneered, biting his words off quietly and deliberately. "Should have killed you when we all were down in that submarine. Lucky for you, my orders were to leave you alive, just put a scare into you and send your infant civilization a little message." He pushed his forehead against Weiss, whispering pure malice. "I'll finish the job soon enough."

"Bazdt. What is this?" The voice was stronger, angrier, thicker with a middle-European accent, but Weiss recognized it immediately.

"Bellona," the man named Bazdt said. "I was just making sure he's fit to go back down." Weiss followed Bazdt's gaze to the front of the vehicle. There she was, framed in the light shining through the lorry cab's doorway.

THE BLACK CITY BENEATH

Weiss was an idiot. He had this coming.

He caught a glimpse of the street, docks on one side. They were back at the harbor, probably not far from where the British navy gave him decompression treatment.

Iris DeHavilland—Bellona, the man had called her—stepped halfway to Weiss, reaching out and slapping the hook-nosed man. "I said one man watches his hands at all times."

She moved with the grace she'd displayed both on the Astraeus and in the hotel on his arm, but there was power and determination in her motions now. She was even more attractive without the rich-and-spoiled act. *Bellona.* She was the enemy.

Bellona smiled at Weiss. "Bazdt, this is not the typical fool we deal with. His family comes from nothing. They became wealthy and powerful because they are deceptive, clever and inventive. Perhaps his father and his uncle didn't teach him all their skills, but we won't take that chance."

She looked straight at Weiss, reading his face intently. Her hair, still cropped short, was black now. "Yes, yes. You do not understand yet." She actually looked sympathetic.

She knelt down, removed a pistol from inside her coat, and slipped it into a sack on the floor. "You hid your family history well," she said. "Even the few who

93

know your lineage think your uncle is your father and vice-versa. I know everything, Karl Weiss. You don't even spell your name correctly, changing the 'C' and the 'Z' at the end so Americans can spell it and pronounce it correctly. It was a fine name as it was, showing your fine Austro-Hungarian heritage." Her face darkened. "At least you chose not to change it entirely, in the name of fame, like the rest of the so-called Houdinis."

A panicked voice called from the front. Bellona stuck her head through the door, barking orders he couldn't quite hear.

Bazdt scowled. "She's led us into a trap. Get ready."

Weiss felt the vehicle slow, the roar of the boiler diminishing. Bellona stepped into the back. Her glare was fierce. "Your meeting with the Supreme will have to wait. But it *will* happen." Everything went dark as Bazdt slid the hood over his head.

The signs had been there on the Astraeus. It was reasonable that Miss DeHavilland had disappeared. Lots of bodies were still unaccounted for, according to the Times. But the quick glances to her hook-nosed "driver" last night, almost unnoticeable as she seized Weiss by the hand, should have set alarms off. She was so genuine.

THE BLACK CITY BENEATH

"You're alive!" she'd exclaimed, squeezing firmly, holding on for just a moment longer than normal. "We must have a drink. I could tell you found me tiresome the other night. Please allow me a second chance?" The man with her had cleared his throat, glancing around nervously. "Busby, you can return home," she said. I'll send for a car later. Get some sleep and have another driver ready."

Years ago when Weiss barely had his sea legs, a sophisticated woman led him to a Barcelona hotel room. He'd awoken with a gun against his head. A man he'd glimpsed on the same promenade where he'd met the woman was busy emptying his pockets. After that, he kept his own men from making the same mistake. Here he was again. A dupe who might scuttle the Navy's plans to—what? He didn't know. He was supposed to be finding that out right about now.

He should have had the good sense to confide in Melville before walking away. Melville was experienced at recognizing deception. This Bellona might still think he and Mulholland were dead, setting herself up for any number of traps. Instead he'd led her right under the nose of the man guarding his room. No doubt that man would be dealt with severely.

Weiss had fooled himself into thinking that he knew people, could see their selfish schemes. But the world was more devious and underhanded than any

R. OVERWATER

salvage diver would ever know. It was hard to admit, but the men and women who tried to hold people like these at bay might well be smarter than him. Melville appeared to be. Maybe his father too.

The vehicle lurched to the left and Weiss fought to remain upright. He felt the rope around his hands shift and he flexed to hide any slack he may have gained.

The vehicle lurched again, this time to the right, and shook violently with the sound of grinding metal. Weiss fell over, banging his head as they screeched to a stop.

A bell, a dull, flat-sounding one, chimed. And then Bellona's voice. "Again." Another chime, and then a sound, like rocks dropping onto a wooden floor. Dust filled his nostrils. There were scuffing sounds and muted bangs followed by silence. Then the squeak of the back panel door hinges. Light filtered through the bag over his head. He flinched as hands seized him.

"It's 'im all right," a man said. "E's alive, too."

Weiss felt the hood coming off and closed his eyes this time, opening them just a little to adjust to the light. Someone was beside him, sawing at the rope. He squinted and Melville's face took shape. "Got you, my friend," the spymaster said. "You're lucky your partner put two and two together."

THE BLACK CITY BENEATH

Weiss stared at the panel his captors had been leaning on across from him. A circular hole, three feet across, revealed another hole through the brick wall the lorry was lodged against. Grit and dust lay across the floor of a cavernous, empty room. Footprints led to an open door.

Chapter 10

High profile meetings were a lousy way to start a day, so Mulholland got up early, had a cup of coffee, and let his mind wander. He took a sip of the black brew while he waited for the others to wander into the strategy room.

Wisps of cloud brushed against the HMAS Mountbatten's window and the room lightened and darkened as intermittent shafts of morning sunlight played through the glass. The sound of attack airships, six of them, fast, nimble and armed to the teeth, occasionally cut through the hum of the Mountbatten's propellers. Knowing the attack ships would escort them all the way the home made him feel slightly better.

Weiss leaned through the doorway, glancing around before walking all the way in. He looked rested—no surprise there. His left cheek was bruised, a new addition to the nicks and scrapes he'd already had when they began.

He was probably more angry than hurt. His gaze was harder than it had been in previous days. Like he was spoiling for a fight. When he saw Mulholland, a smile broke across his face. "The guy who saved my bacon again. I owe you a fishing trip somewhere," Weiss said.

"Make it Cuba. And don't tell any army guys," said Mulholland. "They'll want the same treatment and you'll lose my services. You sure do need them."

Weiss stopped at the mess cart and poured a steaming cup. "Yeah," he said. The smile was gone now—but it had lasted fifteen seconds, a new record.

Weiss pulled out a grey steel chair and sat across from Mulholland, his back to the door. He put an elbow on the table and propped his head up with one fist, staring at him. The engineer could see gears turning.

The master diver looked apologetic as he spoke. "You may have figured out what I think of all this, all these people around us calling the shots."

Mulholland tried not to choke on his coffee. "I'm pretty sure I know."

"Okay then." Weiss took a swig from his cup. "Do you think these spy types and professional liars have as much of a handle on our mysterious enemy as they think?"

THE BLACK CITY BENEATH

"Hell no. And every time they get caught with their pants down, one of us nearly goes belly up. Here's my question to you: If I'd walked out of that restaurant with you at the same time, what would have happened?"

"You'd have been in that lorry with me," said Weiss. "Unless they didn't need you, in which case they probably would have just shot you." He shrugged. "I don't know what to do. Wait 'til we're killed? I pretty much have to follow the orders they give me and I can't say I put a lot of faith in them keeping me alive."

"Me neither," said Mulholland. "I've got a couple ideas but they pretty much depend on *not* following orders. And not asking permission either."

Weiss leaned forward. This might be the first time, Mulholland thought, that he was actually interested in the engineer's opinion.

"Does it involve me trying something an engineer built for the first time ever?" Weiss asked.

"Sort of."

Tharpe appeared in the doorway. Mulholland lowered his voice. "Come find me when we're on base."

Melville, trailing an entourage, walked in behind Tharpe. "Ladies and gentlemen, if you please," said Melville. He gestured towards the large oak meeting table as he spoke, a thick sheaf of papers in his other

R. OVERWATER

hand. "When we land, we will all be getting down to business, so let's make the most of what will be the last time we see each other—until we are either victorious or we fail."

Wilkie entered the room, leaning into Melville's ear and speaking quietly before sitting alongside him. Melville nodded, rising to his feet as Wilkie sat. "Good morning everyone. Major Tharpe." He bowed his head slightly in her direction. "Out of respect to Master Diver Weiss, who has become the unwilling focal point of our mutual enemy's activity, we will begin with the events on the day before yesterday."

Weiss looked uncomfortable as all eyes at the table turned in his direction. Melville continued. "First of all, there is now no doubt that the crew who roughed him up is that of the spy Bellona. She is nipping at our heels and I fear we may see her again before we are ready. It's difficult to tell secondhand of course, but from what Weiss can relate, she may well be Austria-Hungarian and her native tongue might be Slavic."

Melville paused, considering his next words. "This is confusing, as there is no love for Russia from many people of that origin. Then again, depending on what ethnic region you refer to, there is no love there for Prussia either."

THE BLACK CITY BENEATH

Major Tharpe quietly cleared her throat. "If I may, the submarine Mr. Weiss discovered was undetectable by magnometer. They may have already slipped out undetected."

Mulholland watched the various officers mutter to one another. A powerful weapon that blew holes though nearly anything. Undetectable craft, operable at depths man was just beginning to plumb. The helmet—capable of erasing select portions of a man's memory. Who knew what else the minds behind these things were capable of. The Russians were opening a door for them to invade. Mullholland did not feel enthusiastic about the outcome.

Melville was still talking, and Mulholland he returned his concentration to where it belonged. "On another note, we have received word the at least a third of the Prussian fleet is sailing for the coast of Alaska. Apparently the Prussian Ambassador is being extremely tight-lipped, other than to express a general disdain for our intelligence operations so far. Her Majesty is assuming, and rightly I would guess, that the Prussians have little faith in our ability to thwart a Russian advance and are preparing to look after things themselves. There's been no indication that they are actually planning an attack, nor have they ruled it out."

R. OVERWATER

A U.S. Colonel Mullholland didn't recognize spoke up. "They're prickly bastards, the Prussians. But whatever they've got up their sleeve oughtta be more help than hindrance."

Wilkie spoke up. "I'm inclined to agree. Nonetheless, we'd best be prepared to handle this on our own. Roosevelt doesn't want us tipping our hand, which is why the American fleet isn't assembling off the Washington coast en masse." He paused, looking slightly uncomfortable, and pulled a slip of paper from his breast pocket. "At this point, I must reveal that I have not shared all our knowledge with anyone except Mr. Melville, but only because of direct orders from the President and Her Majesty. I will do so now."

He clasped his hands. "We have a man in the field operating beyond the knowledge of anyone in our department. The White House has not given up on this man, and assures us if we found him dead, we'd know he was ours."

Weiss, Mullholland noticed, was paying rapt attention as Wilkie explained. "Our instruction is to apply ourselves to abetting Major Tharpe as plans to neutralize our undersea invasion point unfold. And to watch for any clues that our man is still afoot."

A British commander spoke up. "What about the people behind the technology Russia is borrowing, the ones who are reputed to be searching for a foothold

104

THE BLACK CITY BENEATH

on this side of a sea portal? What do we know about them?"

Mellville looked grim. "Beyond the fact that Master Diver Weiss believes a couple of them are with the Russian spymistress? And examples of their formidable science? Exactly what we have shared with you strategists, Lieutenant Cavendish. Virtually nothing."

It was great to be back in his spartan cabin. Mulholland finished stoking the pot-bellied stove and put the coal bucket off to one side. Now that it was fall, as good as winter to a Kentucky boy, he was happy to see that the coal had arrived. Slapping the black dust off his hands, he heard a knock. The door swung open revealing Corporal Nash, a clipboard under one arm. He tossed Mulholland a pair of googles. "Jesus, it's good to see ya, Chief. Put these on. It's dusty and we're going for a ride."

Mulholland grabbed his old plaid woolen fishing jacket and stepped out to the steam transport chugging a few feet from the cabin. The transport was one of those two-seaters, generally reserved for large skids of heavy industrial material and, like most, devoid of a windscreen.

Nash hopped in the driver's seat and Mulholland clambered up the other side. "You don't have me

105

fooled, Nash." He tapped the clipboard Nash had slid between the seats. "I know a pile of paperwork that needs signing when I see it."

Nash grunted as he slid the transport into gear. "The paperwork can wait." Not a customary statement, Mulholland thought. He braced himself against the doorframe as Nash swerved around a hole.

"No one's going to bother us in here," Nash said. "Between the newspapers, the briefings I'm ranked high enough to be included in, and the fact we're not allowed to communicate outside the camp tells me we are into something deep. Which you probably know lots about." Nash waved his hand. "No need to tell me, I'm not digging. I just have to talk to you about that new process engineer. The one who started the day you left. There's stuff about him that isn't adding up."

Chapter 11

Weiss gripped the handrail carefully as he stepped onto the boat, making sure his feet were centered on the gangplank. He'd convinced the McKinley's doctor he was fit for service, but his ear still rang and his balance still wasn't right after the altitude-induced pressure sickness that hit him on the Astraeus.

It was almost like he was slightly drunk. If they found out, he'd be taken off duty. On another job he might have gone along with that, but on this particular dive Weiss trusted himself at half capacity better that most divers at full. Perhaps that was evidence of some flaw within him. Something to think about if he lived.

"No. Pump assembly and hoses go on *last*," he snapped at a deckhand. He raised his voice over the din of the makeshift loading dock and squabbling seagulls. "This gear needs to be on the McKinley in two hours. Is there anyone here who doesn't know the gear you need to unload and assemble first goes onto the transport last?"

"No sir, Master Diver!" Weiss turned toward the voice coming from up the dock. It was Davidson, the smart-aleck bosun. His hand was outstretched as he lumbered toward Weiss, a big grin stretched across his face. "A pleasure to have you back, Chief. Wasn't lookin' forward to doing this one without ya."

"Good to be back," he said loud enough to be overheard. "Hope you're ready, Bosun. This is the biggest thing the Navy has ever done and we're the guys to do it." Random shouts came from among the crew behind him. Weiss was nowhere so enthusiastic, but no need to tell anyone that. "Now everyone get back to work. And pay attention to the crate with the red stencil on it. Those are my suits. I packed them myself and God help the swabbie that messes 'em up."

He'd bullied his way into being the principal diver so often, using his experience and reputation as the Navy's best to get away with it, that the captain had quit reminding him the Master Diver ought to be up on deck directing the job. Perhaps it was time to start taking heed. But not on this mission. If there were going to be any more surprises, he was probably the most ready. And anyways, he had a score to settle.

The warrant officer, a second class diver, walked within earshot. "Billings!" Weiss shouted.

The officer turned to answer Weiss' call. "Yes sir?"

THE BLACK CITY BENEATH

"You get this loaded up and back out to sea. I've got a few things to finish with the brass and the paper pushers before we sail."

When he stepped off the dock, Weiss reached into his pocket and reviewed the cryptic note an Army officer, Nash if he recalled correctly, had delivered to him in the morning. The corporal had paused after handing it to him, speaking almost apologetically. "My boss told me to say exactly this, and you'd understand. 'Something's not right. Keep your mouth shut and don't trust anyone.'"

Weiss had come closer to laughing than he had in weeks. Mullholland of all people. Telling *him* that. The man was learning. Maybe. He levelled his gaze at Nash. "Understood. So, can we trust you?"

Nash met his eyes, not flinching the slightest. "Deputy Chief Mullholland can." He turned and walked back to his transport. Weiss looked down at the paper scrap. The engineer's scrawl was barely legible. "New development. Maybe. Not sure anyone else would make the right call. We should talk before I come out."

Weiss had pondered the message the whole morning. Mulholland had never been in a bathysphere before. Tomorrow he'd be on one of the trickiest underwater jobs either a diver or an engineer had ever conceived of. So maybe he had cold feet. He

109

ought to. Someone tried to kill both of them and was still out there. That fact had stayed front-of-mind.

Mulholland had proved to be more savvy than the average desk jockey. William Melville and Max Wilkie, two men who were supposed to be on top of the shadowy conspiracy at the heart of this madness—not to mention the Army, Navy, and an assorted pack of England's finest—tended to show after the bullets and beatings. Mulholland might be an over-drinking hayseed, but if he smelled trouble, Weiss was willing to listen.

By the time Weiss got directions to where the engineer was working—a series of portable Army cabins on skids at the heart of a week-old maze of tents, infantrymen and transport trucks—Mulholland was holding court for a group of bigwigs including both Melville and Wilkie.

They were hanging on his every word. They truly thought this crazy scheme would work. But, Weiss admonished himself, it was established that Mulholland was a smart guy. After all, he'd pulled it together when Weiss was stumbling about the crashing Astraeus. Mulholland acted like he'd bought into the plan, so Weiss held some hope.

Mulholland gave a short speech about electricity and metal jewelry, and two privates with sidearms collected rings, bracelets and the like from the crowd.

110

THE BLACK CITY BENEATH

Weiss was clean, so he pushed past the crowd and stepped into the cabin.

Right away the hair on his arm stand on end. A deep hum suggesting unseen powerful forces filled the room, punctuated by the odd small crackle. The cabin, the parts of it that weren't hidden behind of long bundles of thick cables and banks of clean, painted tin cabinets bristling with gauges and meters, was clean to the point of sterility.

Two sets of electrodes on top of a tall cabinet burst into life, bursts of blue energy arcing between them. By now, others were filtering into the room. Weiss could hear them quietly oohing and ah-ing. The sharp tang of ozone penetrated the air.

He didn't pay much attention to the tour. Mulholland's explanations were well rehearsed by now, and Weiss knew the high points: multiple generators with turbines on every river within reach. Miles of cable channeling unheard-of amounts of electricity to an untested device that could make an invisible shield or vaporize attackers, depending on how they chose.

The tour was over quickly. The crowd dispersed in slow gaggles of four or five people 'til only Mulholland remained. He made his way over.

"God, you're healing slow," said Mulholland. "I have to say, your new girlfriend treats you pretty rough."

"Believe it or not, I got the impression she might like me a little, tiny bit." Weiss said. "Makes you feel sorry for any guy she hates."

`"That's the first joke you've cracked since I met you. We must be in more trouble than I thought."

Mulholland looked around and motioned Weiss out the door. It was noon, and the sun had managed to beat some of the clouds back, and noisy, men and steam trucks everywhere, crews pumping handcarts bearing pallets of coiled wire down a makeshift rail line to the bay. He leaned toward Weiss. "I didn't go to anyone with this yet, because so far the only people who've kept our skin intact is us.

I don't know if I'm just paranoid now or what. But this doesn't seem right." They rounded a corner. Past the last tent, about a quarter mile from where Weiss stood, a bluff of trees were shedding the last of their orange leaves.

Mulholland went on. "The day I left, we got this new process engineer by the name of Smith."

"At first, his work came in on time. The boys say he preferred to do it in his quarters where his books were, and that was fine with them. Guess the guy's a bit of a wet blanket. You two would get along. But he

THE BLACK CITY BENEATH

fell asleep smoking, and the fool set the cabin on fire. Burned enough to make it uninhabitable. He and his bunkmate got out, a Private Holstrom. That guy saw him burning his hands to pull a metal steamer trunk out. Thought it was odd, fire was big enough a smart guy wouldn't have taken the chance.

"Next day, Smith had to work in the same spot as the rest of the engineers. Apparently he looks clumsy as hell with a slide rule, didn't turn a lick of real work. Brought it in the next day though. The kicker though, is this."

Mulholland paused as they cleared the tent city, plunking himself down once they had crested a small rise. Weiss joined him. In the distance, the Little Hoquiam River threaded itself through tightly treed banks. "Anyways," Mulholland said, "half the time they need him, they can't find him anywhere. And the night he burned himself, they bandaged him up and kept him in the infirmary. Nurse says he was mumbling in his sleep. Whatever language he was speaking, it wasn't English."

"Huh." Weiss processed the story for a moment. "Two weeks ago, might not seem like much. But now I'm suspicious as hell about everybody and everything."

"That's why I brought you here," said Mulholland. "Take a look at that stand of trees right before the

113

first bend. The water slows there, thought I'd take one last shot at some fly-fishing last evening, maybe clear my head. I didn't go. See the small shiny thing, and that patch of branches that looks cut back?"

It was obvious once Mulholland pointed it out. "I do," Weiss answered. "What are we waiting for?"

Mulholland wheezed as they worked their way through the trees to the riverbank. A small, crude cabin made of crisscrossed deadfall, with an oiled canvas sheet stretched over top, came into view. Weiss could make out two voices, quiet and terse. He tried to pick out what language he was hearing. Russian.

Weiss waved Mulholland in and turned to look back at him. The engineer looked less scared than usual. Good. Weiss pushed through the doorway, confronting the two shocked-looking men on stools with a map between him. The map was of the coast, dotted with red pencil marks.

The men raised their hands. Both were wearing civilian clothes. "Smith, you sonofabitch," shouted Mulholland.

The man closest stood, palms stretched outwards. "Mr. Mulholland. I can tell you everything. I am personally authorized by the Tsarina herself to speak to your immediate superiors. You just have to—"

114

THE BLACK CITY BENEATH

Weiss wrenched a length of tree branch thick as a man's arm out of the makeshift wall and clubbed both men over the head with two lightning-quick blows. They fell at his feet. The supposed engineer tried to rise to his knees, blurting something unintelligible. Weiss clubbed him again and he fell silent, the map crumpling beneath him.

Chapter 12

Mulholland surveyed the empty pallets on the dock, satisfied that everything had been loaded correctly. He could see Weiss at the bow of the cargo boat, the new bathysphere on deck in front of him, as it steamed towards the McKinley. No doubt he was giving the crew the gears about something.

Shaking off the cold, he turned towards land. It had been a busy morning on a grey day. A small nip or two would have helped, but there'd been too much brass on and off the dock for that and he was the highest ranking Army representative on the job. Besides, Weiss' life was riding on the equipment they'd loaded. Actually, his life was too; after all, he'd be taking the second trip in that bathysphere once Weiss got the primary equipment down to depth. Mullholland's heart went out to the guy. Only a few weeks ago Weiss had dove deeper than any man before, in untested equipment no less. Now he was exceeding that depth, again in new equipment.

Mulholland had spent most of the night going over every single rivet, and had welders on hand to buttress any areas that might even remotely be problematic. Weiss had shared the harrowing details of his dive, and Mulholland had slipped in a few more safety features with that top of mind. He'd measured the hatches to make sure a fully suited man could get in and out. He'd also slipped a few secret bits to Weiss.

The brass and stuffed suits of this grand operation were adamant that there would be no trouble on these dives, and they would stop anyone that planned any. Big Bertha shot an angry look at Weiss and Mulholland during this reassurance, their skepticism apparently evident on their faces.

If there was trouble, Weiss would be smack dab in the middle of it. And if that was the case, hopefully the odds and ends Mulholland whipped up with the help of the Scotland Yard lab coats would even the odds a little.

The afternoon, gloomy and overcast as the morning, was spent reviewing the rail cars of materials that would comprise the shield and manned station above the portal. Working round the clock now, the Mckinley's crew would have them on deck by nightfall. The repellent field, enough to block submarines like the one Weiss had explored, would be

THE BLACK CITY BENEATH

deployable in two days. A permanent shield would take weeks. Mulholland hoped they had that long.

"Do you really think this contraption will do the trick?" Nash stepped around from the other side of the rail car.

"Well," Muholland said thoughtfully. "I do believe it will."

"You don't think more tests and a review of a couple more potential designs first wouldn't be smart?"

"Of course. But consider what we're up against, Nash. We've got people from another *world* planning a joint military offensive with Russia. They've got naval technology beyond ours, weapons more powerful than anything we've got and they're already on the offensive.

"Look at the science they use: a conductor that increases the amount of power you flow with the more line you use—with our wires, it's the opposite. And they make a near-indestructible material made from a variation of the same substance—and yet it is unfindable using magnetic detection and conducts no electricity whatsoever. We're outclassed. And all these mucky-mucks that have been tying up my time figure we've only got a few days at best to get ahead of the situation or London, Washington, New York, you

119

name it, will be smoldering ruins before the year is over."

Nash sighed. He slid a rail car door shut and ticked off a box on his clipboard.

Mulholland tried to inject a positive note. "The good news is that a couple days is all we need. If we can control that portal, then we just need to worry about the Russians."

Again, the corporal didn't answer. This time, his gaze was fixed upon the sky to the east. Mulholland turned. Dozens of black specks floated above the horizon, the unmistakable hum of engines now audible. Then it was drowned out by the chug of a steam transport behind them, skidding to a stop so suddenly it threw up chunks of sod only a few feet from Nash. "Deputy Chief Engineer," a fresh-faced private shouted from behind the wheel. "Major Tharpe says she needs you to drop what you are doing and get to headquarters immediately! Hop in!"

Mulholland looked back up at sky, his stomach sinking. "Nash?" he asked. "Where are the crews responsible for getting this shipped out to dock?"

"Crew one is in the mess. Next crew has bunk time, they're loading tonight."

The engineer stepped onto the transport's running board, gripping the passenger handle and swinging himself into the cab. "You empty that mess

THE BLACK CITY BENEATH

hall and kick those other guys outta bed on the double. Get these rail cars to the McKinley right now."

"The higher officers are going to balk at me giving them orders."

A siren drowned everything out. Mulholland pointed at the sky. "Tell 'em to use their eyes and ears." He slapped the dash. "Go!" The driver cranked the transport into gear and they sped away.

The portable cabin serving as headquarters was bustling. The Signal Corps were unspooling hundreds of yards of telegraph wire, running new lines in addition to ones extending from the cabin to a wooden pole, which now leaned under the weight of additional wire. Mulholland stepped aside as a line of officers, mostly Army, burst from the doorway and dispersed without looking at each other. Frantic aides rushed in and out, clutching telegrams and scraps of paper. When he could finally poke his head inside, he was hit by a cacophony of chattering telegraph machines and half-shouting voices.

Major Tharpe and Wilkie looked up from a map as he stepped across the threshold. Their expressions were absolutely dour. "We've been looking for you for over an hour," said Tharpe.

"The siren only sounded a few minutes ago," Mulholland said.

R. OVERWATER

"Never mind that," Wilkie interjected. "This gentleman has news that changes everything."

Mulholland looked in the corner, following Wilkie's gesture. It was Smith, assuming that was his real name, a thick bandage over the top of his skull. He shot Mulholland a glare, then composed himself. "You have me all wrong, sir," he said, his accent much thicker now that he was not disguising it. "Your governments have made a huge," he struggled to find the word, "blunder."

"Indeed we have," said Wilkie. "The Prussians have been spoon-feeding us outright lies. We were never meant to find that flat in London. That was some fancy-footwork from the Prussian diplomat when we caught their lad. Seeing as we had them red-handed, they made it seem like a present to us."

"But..." Mulholland barely knew where to start. "What about the Russian sub Weiss found?"

"A red herring," Wilkie answered. "Deliberately scuttled. Made to look like it sailed under the Russian flag. Those bodies in Russian uniform, placed there."

"The airship that shot down the Astraeus?"

"Undoubtedly Prussian, but disguised as Russian."

"And we're taking this guy's word for it?" Mulholland pointed at the Russian spy who rose unsteadily to his feet.

122

THE BLACK CITY BENEATH

"They're not just coming for you, they are coming for all of us," said the Russian. "I have been following this Prussian *ved'ma's* trail for a year and learned much. Prussia will use this undersea enemy's superior weaponry and divide the spoils. The witch neutralized most of the minds that could have helped you develop adequate defenses in time. It is only now that we have learned their complete plans, and the Tsarina has decided Russia needs help as much as anyone. I doubt she cares about your United States. Or England. But if these others get a foothold up here, they will assemble massive weapons no one can win against."

It was a lot to process, so much skulking and backstabbing. Mulholland had been so oblivious. "I take it Melville is somewhere communicating with England right now?" Mulholland asked. Tharpe and Wilkie looked at each other.

"It gets worse," Tharpe finally answered. "Maybe if we'd figured how to get dependable radiotelephone lines to work across the ocean—"

"We must assume that Inspector Melville is dead," Wilkie interjected. "That fleet of dirigibles up there will be here shortly. Prussian, of course. Our last contact with London Aerodrome said they were under attack. We can assume the base is lost and who knows about the rest of London."

123

The cabin door banged open and an army captain in a helmet stepped halfway through the doorframe. "General Pershing says everyone has to get to the underground HQ right now."

Mulholland looked at Tharpe. "Underground HQ? That's new."

Tharpe stuffed a wad of papers into an attaché case, looking over her shoulder as she headed for the door. "I guess we missed that in your briefing when you returned. You didn't think we'd secure the largest military engineering project in history underground and then run it from tents and cabins up top, did you?

Mulholland followed her and Wilkie out to the waiting personnel car. As the boiler roared to full heat and the car sped away, Tharpe was silent, clearly in deep thought, staring at the dots, now larger, on the horizon. "Bertha?" He leaned in, speaking quietly.

She remained silent for a moment. "This is a first for me. The fate of this whole damn country is in the hands of the Army Corp of Engineers."

He was about to answer when he heard the distant thud of the first bomb.

Chapter 13

Weiss barely noticed the buzz of Davidson's voice in the background, rattling off the depth count of the bathysphere. He'd never seen the point of even beginning until it was deeper than Weiss could swim up from which, in the old days, was pretty deep. Besides, he could tell just by looking out the porthole.

At thirty feet, the colours red and orange disappeared, absorbed by the water. By sixty feet, yellows and greens were gone. Then it was just blues and grays, the outside world growing darker until you were just a lone diver, swallowed up in an abyss of pitch black. Usually, after whatever unpleasantness topside, he relished entering this vast, silent cocoon.

He watched Master Diver Archer, who was clearing the small bunk to take the first nap shift on their two-day dive. For once, Weiss hadn't balked at having a partner with him. He'd been having a bit of a rough patch. Some assistance, and some company, on another miserable job, was actually welcome.

R. OVERWATER

In two days, Mulholland would be down to oversee the main installation. Weiss found himself actually looking forward to introducing the engineer to his world. He'd appreciate what divers went through down here to get a job done.

"Two hundred feet." Davidson's voice was still strong and clear. "Signing off now, Divemaster. I'll come back on when you're ready to set your next depth record. It'll be a big one." Weiss left the bulkhead he'd been leaning against as he watched outside and settled onto the riveted metal workbench, getting as comfortable as possible. He'd be here a while.

The first vibrations were barely noticeable, not enough to snap him to attention. He had no idea how long he'd been sitting there, lost in thought. It was the first time, he vaguely realized, that he'd sat still in days. The memories and unfinished family business Melville had stirred and with it the notion that perhaps it was time to rethink what he was doing with his life. Weiss had just started fumbling towards some sort of conclusion when the bathysphere lurched violently, spilling him and Archer onto the deck.

The lights flickered once and went out. Eerie silence took over as the hum of a dozen small devices and the quiet rush of air from the lifeline to the McKinley ceased as well. Weiss thought he caught the

126

THE BLACK CITY BENEATH

slightest whiff of smoke—a bad sign. The pumps above pulled the air right from the McKinley's deck area and if they smelled any smoke at all, there was probably a lot of it topside.

The earsplitting sound of the atmosphere emergency bell stabbed through the air, pneumatically triggered by the absence of air pressure from the lifeline. Archer swore, his thick English accent barely discernible overtop the din. "This is a hell of a start," he said. "You all right, Weiss?

"I'm fine." Weiss blinked as the emergency lights came on and the sound of the onboard air scrubber whirred to life. There was now officially a time limit before they'd asphyxiate.

Archer flicked a row of switches on a panel behind Weiss. "No sense wasting batteries on the marker lights outside," Archer said. "Nobody will be down here to find us any time soon."

Weiss nodded to himself. He'd handpicked Archer for good reason. "We'd also better—" The bathysphere jerked again, worse this time. The briefest feeling of near-weightlessness gave his heart a jolt, and the first real tinge of fear. With a groan of stressed metal, the bathysphere shuddered, confirming his newfound concern. "Check external pressure," he shouted. "And kill that damned bell."

R. OVERWATER

It was Mulholland's idea to affix an external pressure gauge on the hull. No reason, he said, to rely on people topside for depth, you could calculate that based on the surrounding water pressure. Weiss couldn't recall the formula, but he didn't need to.

"It's climbing to beat hell," Archer yelled over the increasingly louder groan of the bathysphere hull. "We're falling as fast as this soup tin will carry us."

Weiss was already prying back the cover to the emergency air-tank regulator as Archer spoke. "We'll be crushed like bugs in this thing if we don't equalize pressure," said the Englishman.

The veins in his arms popped to the surface as Weiss squeezed the threaded valve of the regulator with everything he had, turning the threaded shaft counterclockwise. It resisted—some swabbie had wrenched it unnecessarily tight—before finally yielding to Weiss' strength. It popped off and air rushed from starboard tank number one. He pinched his nose and blew, the old inner-ear equalization trick—to compensate for the increased cabin pressure. The constant ringing in his one ear came back front and centre. Weiss ignored it as best he could.

"That ought to buy us time," said Weiss. The wrenching sounds of metal subsided to sporadic pops

THE BLACK CITY BENEATH

and pings; normal sounds of a vessel adjusting to new depths.

"Yeah, but it ain't the best use of our emergency supply," Archer answered. "However much time we had, we now got a lot less." He paused. "So. What just happened?"

"Shhh." Weiss held his palm up, silencing him not so much to hear but to think. The sensation of slowing took over for the briefest of moments and then went away. Now, he had the distinct feeling of floating, of bobbing up and down in a current. Normal for a boat on the surface, not down here. He spun the regulator back into the emergency air tank, stemming the rush of air. The panic of the situation was abating, best manage what resources they had as well as they could.

He'd cursed his superiors, forcing him to sit through meeting after meeting, listening to the starched collars and slide-rule jockeys on the trip back from England. But he was grateful now for the nugget of information Tharpe had proposed. Both worlds on either side of the portal had up and down, their own gravity. She'd surmised that there might be a limbo zone between the two where, if they counteracted one another, the effects of gravity would be more or less negated.

129

"Here's what I think," he said, relaying Tharp's theory to Archer. "Who knows what's going on up there. But we're probably floating like a cork in the middle of that hole."

The bathysphere rocked slightly, the distinct bump of something touching it making Archer visibly jump. He reached over, flicked on the outside lights and turned to the porthole beside him, blocking it from Weiss' view.

"I'm the first to admit I ain't seen all God's creations," he said. "But I'm guessing our momentum took us through to the other side. He pulled back from the glass, and Weiss saw an eye the size of a dinner plate. It shone in the light, iridescent, and a thick lid pulled back and forth across it slowly, once. It was no sea creature Weiss had ever seen.

He didn't know where they were for sure. Best guess—they were trapped at the edge of another world with only a short supply of electricity and air. And no way of getting back, at least not without dying from the bends.

Chapter 14

Mulholland was too busy shouting orders at Nash to pay much attention to the confusion around him as everyone scrambled to set up the emergency bunker. Tharpe, Wilkie, two generals and a half dozen officers spread maps across a table. The door at the bottom of the stairs into the room swung open. A shaft of natural light stabbed through the haze, and the whine of the sirens, muted by the foot-thick oak door and 15 feet of earth above them, drowned everything out.

The door slammed shut, every eye in the room turning to the young corporal who entered. He dabbed at a gash on his forehead with a blood-soaked kerchief, scanning the bunker for the leaders. His eyes fixed on Tharpe's table. "It's definitely the Prussian fleet," he blurted out. "Hundreds of them!"

"Well, that confirms it. We've been fools this whole time," Wilkie muttered. "I'll have my resignation into Roosevelt this week. If we survive."

A general stepped forward. "Report, Corporal!"

R. OVERWATER

"They've already bombed the generator at the dam and the two substations upriver, and a squadron has broken off. They seem to be following the high-voltage lines from substation to substation."

Mulholland whirled to look back at Tharpe, already staring directly back at him. The Prussians knew what this installation was here for. They'd been one step ahead since who-knows-when, and it was a good chance they also knew the main installations were now below ground. That meant an attack by land was forthcoming.

"Depending on what stations they get next, we can shunt the power to other stations." Tharpe paused a moment, thinking. "We have to keep power going out to the buoy lines on the water and pray the McKinley is ready. You know what we need to do Mulholland," she snapped.

"I'm afraid I'm not done reporting." The corporal was quieter this time. "Another squadron headed out to sea and only two of our ships are reporting in now. The Prussians went straight for the McKinley. It went down with all hands."

"Well." Mulholland was first to break the silence. "If there's any hope of keeping the Prussian's allies from joining the battle, it rests on keeping this electrical infrastructure intact. The Navy has more

THE BLACK CITY BENEATH

ships, but we only have one line made from this special wire and a handful of generators to power it."

He headed for the door, turning back as he opened it. "I'll be back as soon as I get my men in place. Nash, you're with me. "

The air was thick with airships, with more of the giant craft still emerging in a beeline through the curtain of smoke behind the lead dirigibles. Despite still being a half-mile away, Mulholland could see gunfire arcing back and forth between soldiers on the ground and the airships. Most of the shooting came from the airships. Two split off, their propellers screaming as they drove the airships down, closer to a cluster of men peppering the air fleet with single-shot rifles.

He squinted. Hard to make out the uniform, but it looked like men from the Highland 51st—the soldiers that followed shortly after he'd arrived from England. They'd been forced to take position on open ground between the fleet and the bunker of substation two.

The forward ships were already past generators one and two and the first substation. There was hope; the next logical bombing point would be down the line at substations two and three. He still might be able to ramp up the remaining generators and shunt enough power where it needed to go.

133

The Navy had a second ship with another bathysphere, he knew that for sure, but that didn't mean Mulholland's crews could get power to it. Or that it hadn't been sunk, same as the McKinley. He had to act as if everything might come out right nonetheless. Everything they needed could yet be intact.

It wouldn't necessarily help Weiss. He'd pushed it to the back of his mind in the rush out to the field, but Weiss was probably at least a half-mile down when the attack came. If he hadn't been struck by sinking debris, Mulholland could drop a line and hope Weiss could find it and connect it. Assuming he was alive. Weiss could take a beating. Him surviving, that at least had racetrack odds. As good as Mulholland's chances of getting a ship out there anyways.

A plume of dirt erupted as an explosion struck right in front of the British troops. They fell back several yards before resuming sporadic shots at the airships. The two low attackers, rushing in parallel about two hundred feet up, split apart to reveal a larger, slower airship coming up the middle.

A large shield hung from it, protecting its underbelly. It slowed to near dead-stop, making it a sitting duck, but the Highlanders' rifle fire bounced off it like pebbles. Two slit-doors opened and a black box

THE BLACK CITY BENEATH

the size of a small truck, bristling electrodes, jutted out.

The electrodes were maybe five or six feet thick and 20 feet long. Mulholland's stomach sank as they flashed red-hot and small sparks danced between them. A flash, a thunder-crack—and then he was blind, thrown out of the back of the transport as it slammed to a stop.

His vision swam as the white-hot lightning subsided, spots still dancing in his vision as if he'd stared into the sun too long. Dust blew into his mouth, coating its inside, a hot wind blowing the smell of ozone and charred flesh over him. Nash was already slapping the transport cab with one hand, yelling at the driver. "Turn this thing around! Get us out of here right now!"

Mulholland scooped his spectacles from the ground, setting them in place and looking to where the British men had been. Smoke drifted up. No, that was steam. The ground had been that super-heated, and the vapour obscured his vision. He looked more closely. Small charred mounds were all that remained of the soldiers.

"Chief!" Nash stretched out his hand as the transport circled back toward Mulholland. "Let's get the hell out of here!" Mulholland wasn't going to argue. Moving slow now that it had sacrificed its

135

momentum, the massive death-dealing dirigible was turning in their direction. Smaller ships had slipped behind it, ropes dropping as ground troops lit upon the battlefield. Mulholland could hear them shouting as they pointed toward the main encampment behind him.

The only sound now came from the boiler of their own truck as it turned to pick him up, and the whine of propellers as the Prussian fleet bore down. Otherwise he might not have heard the horn honk behind him, and the shouting of American voices.

"No! Go back!" Nash waved frantically. Behind them was a large personnel carrier, the back filled with the substation crews Nash had assembled in order to man the stations. A squad of U.S infantrymen followed in a second truck. A shadow passed over Mulholland, the sound of airships drowning everything else out.

One of the smaller airships that had first engaged the highlanders spewed a hail of bullets. The transports were easy targets for the massive machine guns protruding from the gondola's nose. A few seconds of deafening high-caliber gunfire and the first truck careened to the left, flipping onto its side and spilling its personnel out the back. Half of them didn't move. The rest scrambled away towards the second truck, still moving. Then Mulholland was blind again.

THE BLACK CITY BENEATH

The crack of the electrode weapon was so close, the ringing in Mulholland's ears drowned out all else. When he could see again, the trucks were blackened husks. Nothing stirred except small tongues of flame darting around the trucks' boiler assemblies.

The one-seater pulled up and Mulholland tried to swing into its box. He'd never chided himself before for the shape he'd let him get himself into, but he sure as hell did now. He had to reach over and take Nash's hand, and the man unceremoniously pulled him over the cargo railing onto the deck where he landed on his face. Sitting up, he could see the driver was aiming straight for the meeting bunker.

Mulholland banged the cab as hard as he could. "Go right! We've got to get to the next substation!" Nash looked surprised. "Corporal, this falls to me and you. We have to keep power running from every generator we can and hope they can get a line down to the primary bathysphere sooner than later."

Nash's face tuned ashen. He looked back at the advancing airships and the soldiers on the ground, and back at Mulholland. A rifle shot whistled past Mulholland's ear and punched a hole through the top corner of the transport cab. They both dropped to the deck, faces pressed to the corrugated steel.

"You're crazy!" Nash bellowed, even though they were practically nose-to-nose. "Those Huns back

R. OVERWATER

there will kill us! If your new buddy is still alive, he'll already be into emergency evacuation procedures. What the hell does one vessel need all that power for? No way, Chief. We gotta get out here."

Mulholland didn't have time to explain. "Listen up!" He could feel his face flushing red. "Are you a corporal in the goddamned U.S. Army or not?"

Nash composed himself instantly. "I am, Chief. Sorry. Just hadn't planned on dying this week."

"I know," said Mulholland. "There's no amount of whiskey I won't pour you when this is over."

Nash summoned a grin. "Whiskey, hell. You're gonna row me to the middle of some lake that's got no water left, there are so many trout in it."

"Forget about trout. Weiss is taking me fishing off of Cuba. I'll make sure there's a seat with your name on it."

Another shot slammed into the transport cab, ricocheting with an angry whine. Mulholland focused on what they'd have to do when they got to the substation. His mind wandered to the weapon he'd just seen. No way the Prussians had that kind of technology before recent. Who knew what else they had up their sleeves? He needed to concentrate and make some smart decisions. This whole damn mission hung on that.

Chapter 15

As quickly as it appeared, the thing outside the bathysphere whipped around and sped away, rocking the craft in its wake. It took a few seconds for the creature's long, undulating body, rough and sawtooth scaled, to pass by the porthole. The thing was massive. Weiss was happy to see it go.

The bathysphere shook again, accompanied by a series of piercing metallic clanks. The sound of grapples, Weiss guessed. Archer looked hopeful. "A rescue maybe?" he asked.

Weiss flipped open a footlocker, digging for the leather pouch Mulholland had slipped him. "I highly doubt it." He extracted a thin of wafer of the black substance. Weiss slammed the locker shut. "Look. No sense beating around the bush. There's a good chance we're going to be tortured and killed."

"Just another day in the damned Navy," said Archer. Weiss could tell he was scared. Only a stupid man wouldn't be.

R. OVERWATER

It'd be a shame to see another good man die beneath the ocean. Whatever Bellona and her superiors wanted from Weiss, they hadn't gotten it yet. Whoever just banged on the hull, they'd be waiting. Maybe they'd kill Archer right in front of him to show they weren't fooling around.

A low, grinding sound tore through the hull and everything pitched sideways, tools and loose dive equipment skidding across the deck-plating, the two divers falling among it. Everything felt heavier as Weiss fought to sit upright; the neutral bouncy on the cusp of the two worlds being overtaken by gravity. He had no doubt which world's gravity it was.

The bathysphere jerked; the distinct feeling of inertia. Bubbles trailed by the porthole. They were being towed. It was almost 800 fathoms to the surface on their side of the portal. Even if they could escape whoever had them right now, there was probably no way to find their way back to it.

So, did he just allow himself to be beaten and killed? No. He owed it to himself to get some licks in. Not just to himself. To a lot of people. The crew on the Astraeus. The great minds whose potential contributions had been erased by that woman and her brass helmet. Everyone who would die as high-minded leaders fought over things that weren't truly theirs to give or take.

THE BLACK CITY BENEATH

There was no way to right it all. They'd probably drag him and Archer out of the bathysphere. If he could get free, get back to it and get five minutes alone, he'd give them one hell of a surprise, courtesy of the Deputy Chief Engineer of the United States Engineering Corps.

"So what's the plan, Dive Master?" said Archer.

"Not sure yet. You do know how things are probably going to go for us?"

"Yeah. I know."

Their momentum shifted. Weiss felt upward motion and got a quick glimpse of structure around them, barely visible outside in the dim light of the sphere's interior emergency bulbs. They couldn't have been traveling more than a few minutes.

"Huh. We're not far from the portal after all," said Weiss.

Archer emitted a low chuckle. "Once we get there, just a short swim up to the McKinley."

Weiss tried to grin himself. "That's the spirit." No sense getting into how the lifeline to the bathysphere might have gotten cut. He doubted the deck of the McKinley was any safe place to be at this moment.

Light penetrated the darkness outside, everything brightening. Weiss could see walls and trusses moving past them, and then the surface of the water retreated down the porthole and they were suspended

141

in blinding light. A familiar swaying sensation, of being suspended by a crane and lowered to a deck, took over. One minor clunk as they landed, and then they were still. Archer reached out and shook Weiss' hand. "Here we go, I guess. Pleasure sailing with you."

The primary lights came on and the instrument panel winked back to life. The men blinked as the dim emergency lights shut off and their eyes adjusted to the regular brightness. Archer said. "How the hell could they know how to hook us up to their own electricity that fast?" Archer asked. "Why would they?"

"They've been ready for every move we've made all along," Weiss said grimly. Maybe not every move. The restored power would make his final job easier—if he actually got the chance.

"Stand away from the hatch! Stick to the sides if you want to live!" The loudspeaker voice cut through the hull, thin and metallic sounding within their chamber. There was barely sound, just a brief breeze as a five-foot hole suddenly materialized in the hatchway, partially cutting through the frame on either side. A thin cloud of metallic dust settled to floor in front.

A man stepped through the doorway, levelling a black pistol at Weiss' chest. He grinned malevolently. "Nice seeing you again." He wore a seamless black

THE BLACK CITY BENEATH

uniform now and had short red hair, but Weiss recognized him: Bazdt, the hook-nosed man.

Bazdt stepped further into the chamber, two men with identical uniforms and pistols stepping in behind him. One motioned toward the divers, uttering a few sentences in a language Weiss had never heard before. He had the same lilting accent of the hook-nosed man, probably cracking a joke at their expense judging by the laughter that broke out.

"Maybe she would. He's pretty, ain't he?" Hook-nose answered in English. "But he's a stubborn one. I bet he gets her so mad, she flushes him out of Chamber Five by tomorrow."

It wasn't just the accent the speaker shared. Both had red hair, which looked strange against their darker, almost-Mediterranean skin. Weiss had been around the world a dozen times over—there was no race of men like this he'd ever seen.

Bellona entered, her sour look making it plain she'd been listening to the men. "You." She locked eyes with the joker. "You pull guard duty first tonight." The man looked down briefly; cowed, but not repentant. Soldiers were soldiers, Weiss thought to himself. You'd find very few who particularly liked taking orders from some foreign woman.

Bellona continued. "By all means, let them escape. I would much rather kill you than these

143

R. OVERWATER

Americans." Glancing around the bathysphere, she shook her head. "Perhaps it's just that I've grown accustomed to the scientific and mechanical superiority of my new home but you are obviously not afraid of risk, Karl Weiss. The dangers you have overcome in these tiny, dangerous toys—no two of this cowardly lot could do it." Hook-nose smiled as her gesture swept toward the two lackeys, bypassing him.

She was most certainly a master of accents. Here, with all pretenses laid aside, her speech was thick with the dense syllables of Teutonic Europe. She sounded like one of Weiss' aunts, back in the old country. She nodded to the trio in black, who circled behind the two divers, prodding them towards the door with their pistols.

Weiss looked over his shoulder as he went. "Do your Russian masters know you aren't wearing their uniform when you're down here?"

"Yes. Russia," Bellona said, ignoring Archer entirely. "We executed that whole ploy well, didn't we?"

Weiss did his best to think on his feet. "You've got time to explain what that means before you kill me."

"Kill you? As I said, you are worth any two men down here—more actually. I planned on killing you,

THE BLACK CITY BENEATH

once, yes. But the plan has always been to have you on our side."

"That'll never happen."

"You are not the first to say that. People change their minds. We can see to it that you come around."

Archer was already through the breached hatch as Weiss stepped up. A dozen or so black-uniformed men stood in semi-circle around the hatch, pistols drawn. A handful of more authoritative looking men and women stood in the back. Many had the same fiery red hair, all had the same greyish complexion. All except one, who weaved his way through the guards.

Weiss recognized the black hair, wavy and thick, combed flat, before he caught a glimpse of the face. The great man himself; master illusionist, cheater of death, the handcuff king, one of the most successful inventors and industrial magnates in present-day America. The one and only Mr. Harry Houdini.

It had been years. Age lined his face, the crinkles around his eyes were new, but he still looked incredibly fit—always a matter of pride with him. Smiling warmly, he looked into Weiss' eyes. "Hello, Karl. I was beginning to wonder if I'd ever see you again."

Chapter 16

Bullets slapped into the thick oaken door of the station bunker and Mulholland strained to hear Tharpe over the base's makeshift telephone line. He'd gleaned all the important details. American troops were on their way to the camp, but most were still one-to-two days away. Highlanders, thankfully, were on base and already fighting their way to the substation to extricate him and Nash. If the door held up long enough.

Most importantly, he was happy to learn the Prussian airships hadn't enough speed and agility to avoid being picked off. The McKinley had probably been lost because the Prussians held the element of surprise. Everyone had anticipated a naval attack by Russia.

Prussia, Russia—it was hard to keep straight. Regardless, the Navy's 14 and 15-inch guns had apparently shot down enough airships, that the rest had pulled back and established a perimeter, likely waiting for reinforcements. Their deadly electric weaponry hadn't proved very effective over the water. The water's conductivity seemed to disperse the weapon's concentrated blast.

The Navy was lowering the other bathysphere in the hopes that Weiss could get to it. That was something.

The Prussian ground assault, however, was more than the encampment had been ready for. Already at Mulholland's door, they would be on the command bunker in no time and much of the camp was evacuating on either flank of the Prussian ground troops. The engineering corps' mission was clear: they had to stay onsite and stay alive long enough get the repellent field radiators near the portal. Closer than originally planned. Mulholland was grateful there was no time to explain why.

Mulholland and Nash would have to reroute the power at the last possible second. Or better, at their leisure after the Highlanders took control of the bunker. Mulholland doubted the odds of that. Bugger.

But, when this was all said and done, he'd have played a heroic part in a major battle. Boy. It was sure going to be fun throwing that in his brothers' faces.

Nash was already stripping off every bit of metal he had; belt buckle, ring, even his leather Army-issue

THE BLACK CITY BENEATH

boots; the lace-holes had metal grommets surrounding them. "What's the news, Chief?"

"Good news and bad news," Mulholland said, following suit. He took his ring off last, after making sure there wasn't even a dime in his pocket. The wild voltages at play in the next room could incinerate a man in a blink if he wasn't extra careful. It was a hell of a thing they'd built, he just wished he'd gotten the chance to revel in the accomplishment. He oughtta be on the front page of every newspaper right now instead of hiding in a glorified dirt hole. He looked up. Nash was still waiting for an answer.

"The good news is the Navy is holding their own." He did his best to muster a grin. "The bad news is that we're with the Army."

Nash unlocked the generator chamber door. "Technically, you're not in the Army."

Mulholland grunted. "Put that on my tombstone, then—He wasn't even in the damned Army.'"

He joined Nash, wrestling the giant wheel around that retracted the huge bolt and together they swung the massive door open. The smell of ozone hit him immediately. He felt the fine hairs on his arms literally stand on end. This was his favorite part of the system.

The whine of train-car-sized turbines drowned out all other sounds, the armatures they drove wrapped in hundreds of miles of fine copper wire, spinning so fast they were a blur. A dense nebula of blue energy coalesced across arrays of electrodes at the end of each turbine assembly. Stray-voltage arrestors, poles of copper alloy with golden globes the diameter of a wagon wheel, surrounded them. The periodic crack of sparks, blue-white lightning as they leapt to the carbon-scored globes of the arrestors, were the only thing audible above the turbines. Some were bright enough to illuminate the room, revealing bare dirt walls and ceiling; testimony to the haste the structures were constructed with. It was eerie. Beautiful.

One need only stand there for a minute to grasp the deadly, unprecedented force they were attempting to harness. Tharpe had shown faith that Mulholland could figure it out, and he had. But, under the gun, he'd had doubts. Weiss' distrust of engineers was not always unfounded. No one had died building these rooms. But Mulholland might have only been one slide-rule calculation off from that.

"Well, better get to it." He slapped Nash on the back. "First thing's first. You'll need to—" A blast shook the room, dust and dirt falling down the back of Mulholland's neck, coating the inside of his mouth as a small cloud enveloped him mid-breath.

THE BLACK CITY BENEATH

His first instinct was to worry about the machinery. Dust was the enemy of electric devices, second only to moisture. Perhaps he'd heard a decrease in the pitch of the whine of turbine number three, indicating a lag in revolutions-per-minute. But if he did, it was momentary and things seemed fine.

His next instinct was to look out the chamber door. Nash was already peering around it. Mulholland could see light around the door now, a robust door that used to seal air-tight, shifted from the explosion. The light flickered, indicating men moving outside, and shouting could be heard above the noise of the generator chamber.

Nash pulled him back in, sealing the chamber door. Mulholland had never seen him use his sidearm before, even in the melee outside. He kept silent on the fact that the corporal had willfully snuck a metal object into a forbidden area. Nash used the pistol-butt to smash away the ceramic coating on the door's inside, revealing the thick oak beneath—the door was not made of steel for good reason. "Stand back, Chief. Bad idea to discharge a pistol this close."

Shielding his eyes with his left hand, he fired two rounds at an angle through the wood into the lock. He flinched as the bullet struck. When he turned towards Mulholland, his pistol hand was bleeding, covered in a multitude of small cuts, slivers of wood protruding from the back of his hand. He holstered the pistol, wiped the blood on his hands onto his pant-legs, and gave the locking wheel a tug counter-clockwise. It didn't budge. "No getting at us now without some hard work. Or some serious explosives." His grin was genuine. "I'll do the same to the next chamber once you're inside."

"Okay," Mulholland said. "If they get past you we're likely buggered anyways, but at the last possible second—" he nodded towards a massive two-handled knife-switch above a bank of dials to his left, "—grab that relay there and throw it. Holler first if you can."

Mulholland took a second to register the finality of it all. "If it comes to that, we're probably not coming back out."

Nash gave him a thin-lipped smile. "I guess not."

Mulholland reached out and shook his hand. "Been a pleasure, Nash."

"Likewise, Chief."

They walked to the next chamber, unlocking the door and heaving it open. Another, louder, explosion rocked the chamber and they stopped to blink away the dirt in their eyes. Terse German voices could be heard over the machinery.

Mulholland slipped into the next chamber. He ducked his head back out before Nash pushed the door fully closed. "One more thing."

THE BLACK CITY BENEATH

"Yeah, Chief?"

"Best reload that pistol once you've got me sealed in."

Chapter 17

Bellona looked over to Harry Houdini. The aging man would know this was a test, and that she was not as easy to fool as the masses that worshipped him. It would be interesting, this little family reunion.

"You would be the foremost expert on our guest of honor," she said. "Suggestions please."

Weiss glared at Houdini. "Look at you. The great man, in charge of great machinations. Just as you like."

Houdini stared into Weiss' eyes, no emotion on the famous illusionist's face. "Handcuff them."

Bazdt led four men, bearing the Supreme Guard's red-slash insignia on their shoulders, up to Weiss and Archer and spun them about. Two yanked the divers' arms back, the other two slapping shackles onto their wrists. Bellona wondered if it was worth the bother. They worked much like the ones in her own world and it was hard to believe Weiss wouldn't know a few of his father's tricks.

R. OVERWATER

"Am I seeing things?" she heard Archer whisper. "Is that Harry bloody Houdini, in cahoots with these bastards?" She swung hard with the flat of her hand, giving him a cuff to the ear.

"We commence the attack very soon." Bellona looked directly at Houdini. "You have time for a brief reunion while you square these men away. I'll be sending the helmet team in shortly."

"Yes, Bellona." Houdini nodded, shoulders slumping ever so slightly before he motioned the soldiers to follow him. His facade slipped for a moment and she could truly see the man's age.

Bellona studied Weiss' face. It was well established he hadn't seen his father in years, hard to know what he was thinking. Greying hair aside, she didn't doubt for a second that you could still shackle and chain him with a dozen locks, stuff him into a milk can, throw him into the river and watch him swim to the surface a few minutes later. But she also knew the physical toll it would take at his age, something Houdini publicly acknowledged when he began his new public life as an industrial magnate and private life as the president's personal spy.

They came to a hatch, Houdini opening it to reveal a room, like nearly everything made floor-to-ceiling of the opaque material.

156

THE BLACK CITY BENEATH

"This whole place is made of that black stuff," said Weiss. "You'd think that—" He was cut short as the guards threw him and Archer to the floor in a corner.

"It is the most amazing, useful substance." Houdini motioned to the walls. "But all this black is rather oppressive. I miss our art, all our books in the old house in New York." He bent forward, looking closely into Weiss' eyes, his voice softening. "Are you all right, son?"

"Son?" Archer spluttered.

Weiss ignored Archer. "You gave up the right to call me that years ago. Uncle Hardeen was more of a father than you."

"And look what became of him," said Houdini. "The threat of anarchists. The world is full of shadowy figures and I had to protect you. After what happened to poor Bess..."

"You don't ever speak of Mother to me." Weiss closed his eyes. He shook his head like a dog shaking off water. "I can't believe this. After you sent me away, you made quite the ballyhoo about serving your precious new country, you great patriot, you. Now Russia is attacking American soil, and you are with them."

Houdini's eyes crinkled at the corners. "Did I teach you nothing after all? The art of well-placed

157

distraction, the days, months, of misinformation necessary for a great illusion? Not the Russians, son. The Prussians. By the time your military realizes the truth they will have lost. But it's all for the greater good."

Bellona slipped back against the wall and watched Weiss' face carefully. He truly believed it. She imagined it would be hard for him to take. Harry Houdini had duped the smartest, most famous people in the world and his son, the one man who should know better, was now in the same boat.

Weiss had the look of a man deep in thought. His situation would be dawning on him. The American navy was waiting for Russian ships that would never show. She knew the Prussian attack was commencing, but whatever had caused the loss of power to his bathysphere would be a mystery to him. Good. She needed him to despair for this to truly work.

"Very touching, Mr. Houdini. But a little tender for a man who's supposedly on our side," said a rough voice from the doorway. Bazdt was here now. The look of hatred Weiss shot at him made her smile.

Bazdt stood inside the doorway, several men and women pushing a large trolley in behind him. Weiss' eyes swept over the windowless helmet on it and she could tell he knew what it was.

158

THE BLACK CITY BENEATH

Bazdt scowled at Houdini. "You may have her convinced, and she may have our Supreme convinced, but I don't trust a single one of you." He looked over his shoulder. "This device, these people here, I do trust. Give me the helmet, let's get on it with it." He flashed a crooked leer. "We'll have you onboard in no time, poor little sonny."

Leaning down to Weiss, he whispered, loud enough for Bellona to overhear. "Hopefully it doesn't work. Then I can kill you." He lifted it above Weiss' head and stopped. "Wait. Let's have Poppa do this, shall we?" He handed the helmet to Houdini.

For the first time, the great magician looked regretful. "Can't be sure what you'll recall of me after this," Houdini said. "I did my best for you. Wish it were I in your place. Escaping the effects of this devilish device is easy as beating a pair of handcuffs if one is prepared."

Weiss opened his mouth in reply, but said nothing. Houdini's eyes narrowed. Then he smiled. "We'll finally be on the same side when this is over. You'll see." He lowered the helmet over Weiss' head.

Chapter 18

Mulholland was dropping his slide rule back into his breast pocket when the third explosion hit. For a moment, he feared the corporal was dead, but then he heard the sounds of magnetic relays snapping shut in the junction cabinet on his side of the door, and the gauge needles on the meter bank to his side leapt into the red, and then back.

Nash had managed to throw the switch in time. All the power on Nash's side of the door was now folding back into this chamber, through backup lines nearest Mulholland.

He'd just confirmed the calculations; there'd be power through the buoy lines—suspended about ten feet below the surface and hopefully invisible to Prussian airships—to power the repellent-field generator until Mulholland had to throw the master relay for the entire bunker. After that, assuming the other generator bunks were still powered up, there'd still be enough electricity for the secondary bathysphere. Worst case, if Weiss made it to the backup, he could wait until the Navy fished him out.

Of course, he had no idea what the ships out there were doing. If they'd been sunk or not. If they were still able to deploy the repellent field. If Weiss was still alive.

He had to be alive. He was down too deep for anyone on this side of the portal to touch him and they'd spent their last night outfitting both Weiss and bathysphere away from the watchful eye of Tharpe to stack the odds a little more in their favor.

Mulholland felt guilty about going behind the Army's back, but Weiss was right; their side was always one step behind. He and Mulholland had experienced too much firsthand proof of that. A few secret precautions weren't going to hurt.

The sharp report of Nash's pistol cut through the generators' noise. Nash screamed obscenities. Three small explosions came in quick succession—grenades, he guessed—and the gauges dropped by half. Damn. Mulholland had hoped they merely wanted control of the area but clearly, they recognized the substation's strategic importance.

With the noise of the machinery in the other chamber dying down, Nash's screams were that much more bloodcurdling. Not the quick scream of a man

THE BLACK CITY BENEATH

being shot or stabbed, but the slow, protracted agony of a man being tortured. Mulholland trembled. The same fate probably awaited him.

He crawled behind a steel relay cabinet just as the chamber door blew off its hinges. Shrapnel spattered the cabinet with sharp pings, some whizzing past and lodging in the support beam beside him. Acrid smoke burned his nostrils and throat.

Dizziness and nausea and confusion seized him as he tried to rise. The concussion of the blast had thrown him for a loop but he made it to the relay switch. It was stiff, and he hung all his weight on it for a second before it budged, a small blue spark arcing to the metal blade as it slid into its saddle. Done. "Best of luck, Weiss," he said below his breath.

The smoke around the door had yet to clear as he crawled toward his hiding place behind the relay cabinet, but he could make out shadowy silhouettes and hear a Prussian voice barking orders. From this vantage point, he could see boots in front of the relay panel.

This was it. He wished he was wearing his wedding ring.

Chapter 19

Weiss heard the snap of couplings as wires were attached, and then the muffled voice of Bazdt. "Now!" A hum vibrated through the helmet, then crackling, and searing, burning agony obliterated all thought. Perhaps he was screaming, but he couldn't hear it. His vision went red. Then there was nothing.

When he awoke, voices filled the room. He couldn't understand what they were saying but knew he was in a different room by the way the sound reverberated. He tried to open his eyes but it was blindingly bright and he could only make out blurry figures. His ear rang at the same level as the day after the Astraeus disaster.

"The Supreme wants to interrogate the prisoners in front of the Council." That voice was Bazdt.

"The Supreme is a fool to bring him into the command center until we know he has been rendered docile." That was Bellona.

"He's not without reason. I can get him to listen to me." And that was his dear father, the master deceiver, the patriot, the traitor.

"If you can't, I'll gladly put a hole in him." Bazdt again.

Bellona's voice was stern. "Not without my orders."

"Don't forget who you answer to," Bazdt shot back. "We don't need the likes of you to crush the weaklings up there in the first place."

"That's because you are a dumb brute. Defeating a nation is one thing. Keeping it and ruling its people is quite another."

Weiss managed to fully open his eyes. Houdini was leaning over him, peering into them. "I think he's all right," he announced. He leaned closer, speaking softly but audibly. "Remember what I drilled into you at age fourteen? What is the combination to my office safe, the one for emergencies?"

"What?" The question made no sense to Weiss.

Bellona and Hook-nose glanced knowingly at one another. "He seems suitably confused," Bellona announced. "Take him to the bridge if you must. But keep a pistol on him. His partner as well."

Weiss struggled to sit up, realizing he was on some sort of cot. Archer was in a chair, head down, hands still bound behind him. Weiss' head swam and

THE BLACK CITY BENEATH

he fell over. Hook-nose grabbed a fistful of his hair. "Here, friend. Let me help you up!"

It hurt like hell. Weiss swore.

"Oh, bit of a tender scalp after the hat, I see." The hook-nosed man chuckled.

"Bazdt! Your keepers will want them in decent condition." Houdini raised his voice slightly. "And we have brought him here to enlist his services, not brutalize him."

"Agreed." Bellona addressed the two men sharply. "Enough. We go."

The walk to the bridge was slow and painful. Accustomed to the unsteady sea, he found his legs quickly enough but that didn't stop the hook-nosed bastard from repeatedly prodding him between his shoulder blades with a gun barrel and shoving him to the point of falling down. Archer wasn't treated any better but remained silent, scowling with his eyes to the floor. Likely, his wrists were as sore and raw from the handcuffs as Weiss'.

The Hjen command center was similar to the submarine bridge Weiss had explored during his first record-breaking descent. Here, there were two daguerreotype maps: one of his world, and another of landmasses he did not recognize.

His thoughts paused. Supposedly, he should be having difficulty remembering certain things. If the

167

R. OVERWATER

helmet had done its job, Weiss couldn't tell. Not yet anyways.

A low-register hum pervaded the room, and the scent was distinct. Some things were universal; all underwater structures stank like the people in them. Every culture Weiss had ever visited smelled different, however, and these people reeked of spicy, sickly sweet perspiration.

Their leader, the Supreme he recalled Bellona calling him, wore a fitted, seamless tan suit. He was taller than most, older, bald and weathered-looking. A half-dozen men and women, similar except that their fitted suits were charcoal-grey, stood around him.

Bellona, Houdini, and Hook-nose saluted the tan-clad man upon entering. He stared at Weiss for a minute, then at Houdini and Bellona. "This is the son you would have run our undersea station on the other side?"

Houdini bowed towards the man. "Indeed. He has overcome every manner of adversity at great depths, and boasts great intelligence and resourcefulness, with my own level of ingenuity and adaptability." He looked at Weiss for a fleeting second. "I will admit, sadly, that in my world he has failed to show ambition for anything greater than his own peace of mind, squandering every opportunity to be a leader. But, as

168

THE BLACK CITY BENEATH

you can see by the small burns on his face, we have treated him. He is fit for service now."

The Supreme stepped up to Weiss, inches from his face. His gaze was piercing, grey irises flecked with red, and he stared into Weiss' eyes for well over a minute. "No." The finality was unmistakable. "I have implicit faith in the abilities of our memory-treatments," the Supreme said. "But I can tell. This one has not forgotten enough to lose his will to oppose us." He turned to Houdini. "Perhaps with guidance and oversight, he could serve as ably as you have. I would like that—you have been indispensable in our plans and your service assures your freedom once the Prussian canon-fodder has fulfilled its role. But I cannot take any chances with this one."

He pointed at Bazdt. "Take them to the aft airlock. If we were closer, I'd have you see to it that they floated up where they could serve as a message. But seeing that we begin a critical assault shortly, I'd prefer them gone immediately."

His gaze shifted to Houdini. "What's the expression you use up there? 'Loose cannons?'"

"Indeed, your Supremacy."

The Supreme's eyes hardened. "And do you have an issues with me executing these two men."

169

R. OVERWATER

"None whatsoever. It is a shame, I admit, but it is critical we remain focused on the greater good that will come from your plans."

Weiss stared at Houdini as intently as the wrinkled leader had. He saw no trace of emotion. Just blind compliance. Perhaps that damned helmet had truly affected the old man, but he wasn't so sure. Ever since the government had drawn him into its shadowy politicking, reapplying his mastery of deception and escape to both spy and train spies, he'd been a different man.

But Harry Houdini—Erich Weisz to his family— had no love of tyranny. The family had originally left Austria-Hungary for good reason and the great entertainer had been old enough at the time to remember what they'd fled. It was difficult to believe this father, cold and faulty as he was, would support the butchery that was coming.

Bazdt shoved Weiss over beside Archer, chuckling just loud enough for them to hear. "Looks like I get my way for once," he said under his breath. "How long can you hold your breath, boys?"

He called two men over, who spun the divers about and prodded them toward the bridge hatch.

"Wait." The Supreme pointed at Houdini. "He's as able as anyone with our machinery. Have him

THE BLACK CITY BENEATH

discharge them and report to me on how he handles it."

The hook-nosed man smiled hungrily. "And if he tries to stop it?"

"I trust him. But in the unlikely event, shoot him and send him out too."

Houdini approached the hatch. "I will not fail, rest assured. But I'm nowhere near as fit as these two, I'd feel better being armed this close to them."

"Give him a weapon." Bazdt looked displeased at this, but motioned for a guard to hand over his pistol.

Stepping back, Bazdt, seized Houdini's arm and steered him forward. "All right, executioner," he said, still speaking quietly. "It's your show, wizard. Please foul it up, nothing would give me greater pleasure."

"You need not doubt my intentions," Houdini answered. He looked at Weiss, making eye contact and then looking away. "I can be trusted." He waved at Archer with the pistol. "Both of you, single file. You first."

Weiss stepped into line behind Archer. He could see the British Master Diver's hands for the first time—they were soaked with fresh blood, up and down his wrists as well. It was obvious he'd been straining against the cuffs.

They walked several hundred yards. Whatever vessel they were in, it had to be massive, much larger

171

than the red herring, the submarine Weiss had "discovered". They descended a winding grey steel staircase and entering a bay with several, small, ovoid craft perched on mounts. One sat by the bathysphere at the edge of an open bay, with a clear top hatch sitting wide open.

The room was round, ringed with portals offering a 360 degree view of the water outside. Smaller sarcophagus-shaped vessels were mounted on the walls, emergency escape vessels, Weiss guessed. Larger, four or five seaters, were attached to the wall, hatches open same as the other vessels. A single red button, one of the few things contrasting the omnipresent black and gunmetal, dotted each hatch frame. Weiss surmised that the round bay must actually extend below this deck, as there were four unoccupied airlocks at the 45 degree marks.

They'd need to open one, maybe prepare it. He'd have to get these cuffs off while they were doing it, and prayed they had something resembling a traditional American lock keeping them shut. He needed thirty seconds and a little luck. But... He looked at Houdini. *C'mon, old man*, he thought to himself. *Tell me you haven't changed that much.*

Bazdt strode ahead of the crew, approaching an airlock as Houdini and the two other guards pushed the divers around the bay edge behind him. When

172

THE BLACK CITY BENEATH

they came between the bay edge and the open craft, Archer suddenly dropped back beside Weiss and whispered in his ear, "Follow my lead."

"Hey, you! Step back up!" A guard slipped past Weiss, seizing Archer's shoulder. And then Archer's bloody red hand, his left, was around the soldier's throat. His right fist came up hard from below, landing under the man's jaw as Archer pitched him into the other guard.

"No, wait," Houdini yelled.

Archer bowled the two over bay edge into the water. When he turned back, he held one of their pistols, eyes darting around the room for the third man.

Houdini gave Weiss an urgent look.

A decision had to be made. Weiss went with his gut. "Listen to him," he yelled.

"No offense," Archer shouted back. "But he's crooked as a dog's hind leg and you're barmy from that helmet." He circled Houdini and Weiss in his brawny arms and shoved them down on the floor by the small undersea craft. "And it's too late anyhow." He peered over the top. "Now, where'd that ugly one go?"

Was it possible to fire one of those black weapons in such close quarters? Weiss got his answer as they heard boots clambering up the ladder on the other

173

R. OVERWATER

side of the craft. "Don't let him get up top, Archer!" Weiss yelled.

Archer ducked, pressing up to the hull underside. Thankfully, the bottom half of the craft was increasingly tapered as you approached the keel— same as any boat. From a higher perch, Bazdt would be able to fire downwards. A hole in the deck would not flood the compartment for the same reason the open bay didn't—the air pressure. He'd have a clear shot the second anyone stepped away from the protection of the under-hull.

"You may as well come out now, poor little topsider boys!" Bazdt's voice echoed throughout the bay. "It won't be long before I get some help!"

Trying to dodge pistol shots while running with his hands cuffed was a frightening prospect. He wouldn't be running so much as waddling. But if he made it to the bathysphere, Weiss could kill three birds with one stone—the first being that he would likely distract Bazdt long enough for Archer to take a run at him. Quick thinker, good fighter, that Englishman. If only he'd consulted Weiss before he made his move.

He cleared his head; the time to go was now.

Leaping out towards the bathysphere with all the speed he could, he took a series of long strides, weaving left and right. Weiss heard a Hjen pistol

THE BLACK CITY BENEATH

chime. He didn't look, focusing only on the open bathysphere hatch. And then he was through it, out of Bazdt's firing line.

Even if they got out of here, getting home was a near-impossibility. But, the brass up in Washington would be pleased to know that Weiss was about to advance them that much closer to success. Just not in the way they had planned.

Chapter 20

Bellona stared at the Supreme, watching him dismissively send two perfectly good men, merely misguided as the good ones often were—away to their deaths with nary a thought. His skin was sallow, yellowed, wrinkled, wrapping a weak, diminutive frame that only could have risen to power through birthright within the cliques of this horrendous, claustrophobic city.

He spoke quietly, his council gathered around him, unselfconscious with the same self-bestowed authority and infallibility the so-called great leaders of Europe had. That trait drove her loathing the most, fanning years of burning contempt into an inferno of hatred.

That hatred made her actions not-so-different from theirs. She was painfully aware of that from the first day she pledged her service of Austria. How many innocent men and women had she killed to prove she was the perfect loyal subject? How much killing in just the two years since she had wormed her way into

R. OVERWATER

this undersea world's invasion plans? How many scientific advances had she denied to her own world by nullifying the memories of great, innovative leaders who usually just wanted the best for humanity? It didn't matter how many.

Every person she had ever killed, every brilliant mind she had ruined with these under-dwellers' awful device, it would ultimately spare that many more. Now, there was just a little more work to do.

"Your Supremacy?" She waited for him to give her his full attention. He waved his council quiet, folding his arms with the expectant look she had so grown to loathe. "I have identified certain things within the American craft both your scientists and your council should be aware of." There was no reason to doubt her.

He spread his hands, looking impatient. "Let the scientists report on it."

"I do not think these decisions should be trusted to them, I'm sure you will agree when you see it. They are not up to the same level of decision-making as their leaders."

He nodded. "Very well, then."

"I will make sure Bazdt and Houdini have completed their executions and everything is ready. Join me in the auxiliary launch bay shortly."

178

THE BLACK CITY BENEATH

She walked out. Hopefully she had missed the killing of Weiss. Not that she wouldn't have done it herself if she had to. But with any luck, he would be the last innocent martyr in her plans. And, against all odds, those plans had gone well, hadn't they?

The Prussians should be in control of the American beach by now, awaiting contact from the Black City. The Hjen under-fleet would be nearing the portal. She pulled a watch from a pocket on her sleek coat. A little longer and they would be through the portal, too late to turn back. Then, it would be time.

Bellona rounded the corner, entering the bay. Immediately she ducked back, and peered around again. The sweaty Englishman lay facedown, dead or unconscious, beside a rec-sub. The two guards who had accompanied Bazdt were also dead, the upper torso of one obliterated by a Hjen weapon. Both corpses, for some reason, were soaking wet. She saw Houdini, half hidden by the sub, holding a pistol and shaking in the after-moments of the shooting.

Weiss came tumbling backwards from around the side of the sub, falling as Bazdt delivered a high-flying kick to his jaw. The fighting arts of Hjen officers were something to be reckoned with, similar to the skills taught in the Orient, and she had witnessed Bazdt use those skills ruthlessly, beating countless men to bloody pulps at her command. Frankly, she would

R. OVERWATER

rather see Weiss be shot than die the way he would die now. But he and his partner were both somehow out of their handcuffs. The man did have an uncanny knack for cheating death.

Bazdt jammed his boot-heel into Weiss nose, which already gushed a steady stream of blood. Weiss managed to get up on all fours, only to receive a kick to the midriff. He coughed, spat a mouthful of blood, viscous with saliva, and fell again. Bazdt allowed him to rise to one knee, before stepping in and driving a vicious punch to the side of his head. Weiss managed to partially deflect the blow with the back of his hand, but in doing so fell back on his haunches.

He was exposed and weak. Now would come the final onslaught Bazdt was famous for. The demonstration of his true prowess always came in a final, finishing flurry of blows no one could withstand. Bellona allowed herself a momentary pang of dismay, then pushed it into the place where she kept such sentiments.

A shame, really. Had Weiss prevailed, and moved quickly enough, she could have let him escape without jeopardizing her master plan. Upon closer look, Bazdt's bottom lip was split, and the side of his face was beginning to swell and discolor. Impressive: few men ever landed a blow on her second-in-

THE BLACK CITY BENEATH

command. But merely landing blows wouldn't be enough, alas.

"And here I was looking forward to fighting you," Bazdt taunted. "Should have known you wouldn't be up to it. I should have given you a weapon to even the odds."

Weiss spit another mouthful of red. "No need," he coughed. "I'm alright. Just wanted the pleasure of punching you in the face a few times before I killed you." He clutched his stomach and rolled over onto one knee again, facing away. Bellona could see something in his hand now, out of Bazdt's line of sight.

Bellona bit her lip, stifling habits developed over the past year. Bazdt was a cold, repugnant thug, but he'd proved indispensable. On any other day, she would have warned him. Or, if need be, stepped in and shot Weiss herself. But not today. It was a rare thing, letting an event play out to its own end.

Bazdt danced to one side, circling Weiss, looking for the best line to deliver the finishing blow. "You're a tough one, I'll admit that. But you're obviously not trained in hand-to-hand combat."

Weiss had his feet under him now, hunkered down with one palm on the floor for balance. Bazdt leapt into the air in front of him, hand extended for a chop to Weiss' neck. "There's no way you *ever* could have beaten me in a fight."

Weiss grunted as he shot to his feet. "Yeah. That's what I figured too." The diver's body tensed, the veins on his neck popping out, the sheer physicality and strength of him apparent as his arms joined in front, giving Bellona a clear view of the object he was pulling from his pant waist. She recognized it instantly; a U.S. Navy-issue dive knife. Thick and strong enough to be used as any number of tools, sharp enough to pierce the rough hide of a shark.

The blade caught Bazdt just below the sternum, continuing up to the middle of his chest as Weiss drove upwards, both hands wrapped around the knife hilt, with all the strength of his arms and legs together. The force of his attack lifted Bazdt over his head, and every muscle in his arms stood defined.

For a second, arms in the air, he stood defined like a sculpture. He was magnificent. A born fighter, yet a reluctant killer. If only more men were like him.

A loud gasp escaped Bazdt's lips, followed by coughs of pink froth. His eyes were already going dim as Weiss threw him to the floor, giving the Supreme's henchman a clear view of Bellona standing in entryway shadows. Shock registered on his face as he realized she had been there all along. His eyes pleaded. Then the dry, hollow look came, the dead

182

THE BLACK CITY BENEATH

man's gaze. He was gone. If today went as planned, she no longer needed him anyways.

She watched the escape dispassionately. It was a pity about Weiss and his brilliant father. The latter had not been as clever as he had thought; she knew what he had been up to in his free time. She would have counted these men as allies had things been different. Perhaps she should stop their foolhardy exit. They deserved to live. But the final minutes were upon her. She was too close to stop now.

Chapter 21

The guilt was fleeting. In the seconds it took to slap Archer into consciousness, Weiss wrestled with the fact that he'd just killed a man. For the first time ever.

Really though, he had to kill him. No way around it, and a good chance innocent people might live because of it. Besides, if anyone ever had it coming from Weiss, it was that man in particular.

He looked at his father who appeared equally distressed as he made his way over. He'd been armed and he must have shot the first two guards as they crawled from the water. Archer came to at that moment, bolting upright, eyes wildly searching the room. "We've got to go!" He leaped to his feet, unsteady only for a second before pulling Weiss along.

Weiss followed his lead, heading for the larger multi-personnel escape pods. The clock was ticking. They were dead men for sure if they stuck around. He swiveled his head as he climbed in beside Archer. "Come on!" he yelled at Houdini.

"Forget the bleedin' traitor, Weiss," Archer said, his hands combing the control board as he searched for a way to launch.

"He's with us," Weiss shot back.

"You're still daft from that damn helmet. We've got no time to argue."

Houdini reached in and grabbed both men, his eyes imploring. "No, not this way! You have to follow me!"

Archer swatted him away. "Your fair-haired boy 'ere can stay if he likes."

Archer was probably right—Weiss knew they wouldn't live another hour if they stayed. "Old man, you've got to come with us." He grabbed Houdini's lapel, overpowering his efforts to resist. Punching the red button on the door frame—best guess was that would initiate an emergency deployment sequence— he pulled Houdini in, reaching up with his other arm and pulling down the hatch.

It clacked shut, spring-loaded bolts thumping loudly as it locked tight. The sound of compressed air through tubes swelled up, and in a whoosh of bubbles they shot away into the ocean.

Archer and Weiss were silent as their view filled with the expanse of the Black City. Small submarine bays stood in a vertical column above the one they'd just fled. Tier upon tier of black, oblong discs, stacked

THE BLACK CITY BENEATH

up a half-dozen at a time, stretched out in rows as far as they could see in the inky water. Lights blazed and blinked, giving depth to an underwater city no earthly sailor could ever imagine.

Archer broke the silence first. "Anyone who could build this, they'll give Her Majesty's navy a run."

"It is impressive," Houdini answered, quietly, his voice heavy with resignation. "Self-contained. They get their oxygen through hydrolysis—running electric current through water to separate the oxygen and hydrogen. They are truly advanced beyond us. And they've been giving hydrogen to the Prussians to help build a big enough fleet to control the civilized world."

"You mean Russian," Weiss corrected him.

Houdini sighed. Weiss could now see a weight had settled on him since they last spoke. "No. Not the Russians. You've been had. Perhaps we've all been had."

"You'll pardon me if I can't take either of you seriously," Archer said.

"We can trust him." Weiss looked past them both trying to see through one of the ports. He had no idea how deep they were, the first glimmers of light would indicate they were approaching the surface. And whatever awaited them there.

"I should have known right away, I guess," Weiss said. "The more convincing he is, the more likely he's

187

playing you for a patsy. I've watched him plant red herrings days ahead of an act in order to set it up. He pulled a great one a few years back. Fooled Roosevelt himself into thinking he can truly do magic."

Houdini gave a half smile at the memory.

"But it's always deception and subterfuge with you, isn't it? I could never tell the father from the man playing a father." Houdini's smile faded. Archer stared at Weiss, still not making sense of it all.

"Anyways," Weiss directed this at Archer. "Assuming that helmet didn't make him forget everything, I figured he was up to something when he handcuffed us. He knows perfectly well I could get out of those faster than he could by the time I was twelve."

Weiss slapped Archer's shoulder. "By the way, good job on getting out of them yourself. Flexing when they clamp them on and using your own blood to slip out of them is the hard way—but at least it works."

Archer beamed for a moment. "All well and good, but did the helmet fry your noggins or not?"

"In this case, burns aside, it posed no serious risk," Houdini answered. "I despaired actually, until I saw that sliver of conductor when Karl opened his mouth. Anything conductive in the mouth, metal teeth for example, disrupts the current they use to target the memory portion of the brain. Myself, I kept

THE BLACK CITY BENEATH

an inch of copper wire under my tongue. Barbaric device, even when it works. Too imprecise. Some men merely forget years of research, I've seen other become jabbering idiots."

"But my original point," Houdini continued, "is that the Prussians have been in cahoots with this nefarious society the whole time. That woman and that dead brute back in the submarine bay have been wiping out new science to make us easier to conquer and control by the Hjen. They posed as Russians to throw the scent off Prussia. And the Kaiser is deluded, I might add, if he thinks these evil monsters are going to keep their end of the bargain."

Archer pointed to the porthole across from him. Light was beginning to filter through the deep water.

Weiss knew exactly what Archer was thinking. "Well, you still need to tell me how you ended up with these people, why Wilkie and Mellville don't seem to know where the hell you are," he said. "Basically, you still need to convince me you are one hundred percent on the up and up. But now is not the time, we'll be at the surface soon."

He pulled out his dive knife. Blood had dried on its hilt. "We're either going to have to fight or, hopefully, run and hide right away."

The down-beaten look Houdini had when he'd entered the craft settled onto his face again. "No, son.

We'll do neither. Our trip ends here, unless we go back to the Hjen city."

He looked upward as he spoke. "The world up there is in its death throes. The air is unbreathable. Only small communities remain, eking out a life in the wreckage. The Hjen, the more advanced culture, have made a material impervious to this, the Opace, and that's one of the reasons they build nearly everything they have from it. They have prospered in a fashion but their days are numbered too.

"The ocean portal is their second attempt at breaching the divide to a new world. I've seen their scientists' documents; the technology is a variation of the same used in their weapons, but beyond my comprehension. Their first one, in the air, was built out of greed, a search for places to plunder. Immediately, a poisonous atmosphere entered through it, slowly killing this world. They retreated underwater. Other societies were not so lucky."

Archer crawled from his seat past Houdini and started rummaging through a series of lockers behind.

Houdini ignored him. "The city we just fled, despite being beyond anything our world has been able to build, is temporary at best. The ocean we are in is this world's last. Once it covered a third of the

THE BLACK CITY BENEATH

planet. It grows smaller every year, threatening their home and the only source of the air they breathe."

"So they need a new world to inhabit, and their science gives them the upper hand in ours." Weiss thought it through. "Still, tough to pull off without allies on our side of their portal. That explains the Prussians and that evil wench. And we still might give them a run for their money, so that explains the helmet and our scientists."

Houdini smiled, puffing up a little. "Well. There's no room in that city that can keep the great Houdini out, and no secret they can hide. They are completely oblivious to how much I know, more than anyone. The Prussians will get theirs when dominion over the earth is established. They intend to dispose of Bellona as soon as their North American base is established."

"Bingo!" Archer exclaimed, pulling out a pile of cloth bags and lengths of shiny grey hose and piling it on the deck behind him.

Weiss stayed focused on Houdini. "Go on."

"I have been though her chambers and secret hiding places. I haven't discerned her real name, but it is not Bellona. That name is actually the Italian word for 'fight.' And wherever her allegiances may be, it is with neither the Hjen nor the Prussians. I've discerned that much, but not what she is up to." He

191

R. OVERWATER

tapped his temple. "Probably up here where it can never be found. She is a diabolically clever woman."

It was a lot to make sense of, but there was little doubt what the old man was saying was true. If anyone could catch the master deceiver in a lie, it was Weiss.

"Okay. That makes enough sense. But explain to me how America's greatest entertainer-turned industrialist ends up at the table of a man who intends to rule our entire civilized world."

Houdini looked sheepish. "Well. After I patented the altered Mark V dive suit, the first a man could shed in an emergency, it occurred to me that my talent of designing and commissioning the construction of clever devices could well be the path to a normal life. One that did not include engagements every night around the world. And so I pursued it, but it turned out to be a ruse more than my life's work."

Archer cut in. "Gents, If I may. I think I've solved our breathing problems when we break surface."

Weiss looked at the pile Archer made. Everything was still disassembled in component form, but he recognized it: self-contained dive suits, identical to the ones his assailants wore when he first discovered that sub. "Good job," he answered, motioning for Houdini to continue.

192

THE BLACK CITY BENEATH

"You were young, you likely don't recall my first sold-out engagement in London, where I finally began cracking the European market. William Melville, who was still just superintendent of Scotland Yard, had yet to form MI5. But he and the U.S. Secret Service's Wilkie saw in me an excellent spy whose skills could bring the forces of good whatever secrets they might need to uncover."

It was a bit much, the flowery description of colonialists, empire builders and war-makers as the "forces of good," but Weiss didn't interrupt.

"It turned out, despite the fact my business flourished, that it would just be a cover for years of espionage. I was reluctant, but who better? There is no lock that can keep out a true Houdini, or the many agents I have since trained. No secret that can be hidden."

Houdini's look softened "Attempts on my life, and your poor mother's, started almost immediately. You can see why we gave you to your uncle to raise as his own. When they—" He hesitated. "When anarchists bombed Hardeen's performance in London, it was only because they believed he was in league with me."

For once, the family patriarch didn't look full of self-confidence. Weiss could barely recall such instances. Houdini looked contrite, apologetic; not

193

qualities Weiss had ever associated with his estranged father.

"I never meant for you to grow up as you did, son." Houdini looked Weiss up and down. "But look at you. You are fit, smart, strong, capable and you possess a conscience almost to a fault."

"Well." Weiss jammed a surge of emotion back down were it belonged. "Mother would be happy to know we'd talked, I suppose."

"Beg your pardon, men," Archer said. "Hate to interrupt a tender family reunion, but I for one don't plan on this being the end." He shoved a mound of dive gear towards each of them. "When we hit the surface, any minute now I'm guessing, I say we strap this stuff 'ere on and head to the first hiding place we can find."

"It'll do until we can come up with a plan." Houdini met the eyes of each man levelly. "I have colluded with the enemy, and the evidence against me will be overwhelming. If we make it back, I'll hang if I fall into any hands that aren't American. But those are slightly better chances for survival than if I stay here. You can count on me."

Weiss believed him. And that was truly something. He braced as the escape pod bobbed to the surface. Looking through the glass, all he could see at first was brownish-orange sky. The light was

THE BLACK CITY BENEATH

flat without visible clouds or sun. The dreariest sky he'd ever seen.

Archer handed Weiss a mouthpiece, something resembling rubber, with a long hose trailing to a canister. Weiss cracked a spigot on the canister's top and Weiss heard the hiss of air. Putting the mouthpiece between his lips, he took a deep breath. It tasted foul but the air was breathable and he gave a thumbs-up.

"'Your lad's in charge of this mission," Archer said to Houdini. "I say the leader can pop out and take a gander first."

Weiss wrenched the large hand-latch at the canopy frame to the open position. Archer, grabbing a mouthpiece, nudged Houdini, urging him to do the same. Pushing the hatch up and open, Weiss stood up and took his first look—one of mankind's first looks he realized—at another world. His eyes burned from the air.

Clearing his vision, the first thing he saw was a dilapidated building on a hillcrest approximately a half mile away, a dock attached to it. A skeleton of girders poked through the crumbed rooftop, rusted and pitted beyond use.

The next thing he saw, as he shifted his gaze from the shore to the ocean behind him, was Bellona, standing in a larger craft, canopy lifted to the side, a

195

rifle levelled at him. She pulled her own mouthpiece out, letting it dangle against her skin-tight dive suit. She looked amused.

"Congratulations on surviving your execution, Mr. Weiss." She took her left hand off the rifle-stock just long enough to reach down into the craft. With a whirring sound, her small sub began to inch towards him.

"Now, let's talk about whether you'll live to make the trip back down.

Chapter 22

***Fools*, Bellona thought.** Brave ones, with an admirable combination of skill and luck, but fools nonetheless. Bellona could hardly believe Weiss had successfully blundered this far. If he had known what he was stepping into the day he set foot on the Astraeus, would he have continued if he wasn't under orders? Probably. He had a fool's idealism. So did she, in her own way.

And the Kentucky hillbilly too. Based on the last report, the Prussian invasion was going as planned. There'd be little doubt that he'd be among the charred dead littering the battlefield at the American camp.

She'd kept her distance as she negotiated the three in the escape sub, knowing full well they would seize any opportunity to best her. For the moment, she no longer needed to kill them. Maybe she wouldn't have to at all.

There was no reason to trust her and when they'd finally agreed to climb into her craft, they were just

R. OVERWATER

buying time to find a better escape method. Wouldn't they be surprised?

"I know how methodical you are," said Houdini. "You would never have chased us alone if you didn't have your reasons."

He was right about that. The less she talked, the easier it was to pilot the saucer-shaped sub while keeping her rifle pointed across the cabin.

"This thing is pretty fast," Weiss said, craning his neck to see outside the bubble as they approached the sprawling undersea city. "I was wondering how you'd managed to beat us up there."

"Now you know." The sub slipped into the stanchions outside the launch bay and Bellona allowed herself a quiet chuckle when her prisoners fell over as the hatch slammed against the airlock.

Weiss followed the motion of her rifle barrel, opening the hatch and spinning the release on the airlock. He looked deflated as he turned behind him. "Coming back here is pretty much the end of us. Just so you know." Houdini shot a puzzled look at Archer.

Poking his head through the lock first, Weiss raised his hands, and stepped through. The other two looked at Bellona. She waved the rifle in answer and they followed, Bellona stepping in behind them.

Excellent. Only two guards had their rifles levelled as she stepped into the bay. They relaxed theirs upon

THE BLACK CITY BENEATH

seeing Bellona. Across the bay to the left, the Supreme and the council stood over the body of Bazdt. Some walked about, surveying the aftermath of the fight.

The Supreme's gaze was piercing. "There you are. When my most trusted man is dead, I expect to be notified."

"I was not here in time to save him. But I was in time to catch the prisoners. One does not get results stopping to weep for the dead."

The Supreme was incapable of smiling, she suspected. His expression now was as close as he'd ever come to that. He addressed his council. "And that is how an other-worlder became my most valued weapon. We are fortunate they have few like her, and that she has joined the inevitable victor."

There were few like her, true. He was right about that.

The council was standing close to the Supreme. The guards were in her immediate field of vision, their attention still on her prisoners. About a sixty-degree radius; quite manageable. Savoring the moment, she allowed herself this, just for a second. She nonchalantly brought her rifle barrel up.

The armed men had to go first. She doubted she missed their hearts by more than an inch as her rifle pinged and chimed, eliminating her victims one by

199

one. Unlike the Hjen soldiers' regular armaments, carving out broad, clumsy holes, her rifle was a precision instrument, built to the specifications of Bazdt, who had been an even better sharpshooter than she.

Only slightly better, and he had been the best. Now she was the best, and the councilmen and women slumped dead to the floor one after another. "Not so fast, Herr Weiss!" He froze in his tracks, already close to the far exit in the mere seconds she'd diverted her attention.

And now the Supreme was attempting to slink away. A shot to his knee ended that quickly enough, and she put one through his shoulder to cripple him further. In the early days, being so cruel was merely part of the disguise. It came easily now.

She wasn't necessarily disappointed in herself for that. She was a product of men like the Supreme, men like Houdini and Archer even, blind followers of power, oblivious to the ruined lives such power was made of.

"On your knees, children!" The trio complied and she stepped around them so they and the Supreme were in her line of fire. She paused. Why was Weiss looking at the American bathysphere instead of her? He had to know by now she was still willing to kill him—she'd prefer not, but nothing was going to get in

THE BLACK CITY BENEATH

her way and he seemed smart enough to recognize it. Almost as if he didn't care... Odd for a man who'd fought so hard to stay alive so far.

"You are throwing your future away!" The Supreme's eyes were both pleading and disbelieving. "And damning an entire people to a slow, choking death."

"Please." She could not have felt any more contempt. "I'm showing you the same compassion you have shown to all the people on your surface. And we all know which society consigned this world to its terrible fate, do we not, oh exalted Supreme?"

He never answered, falling on his face dead as Bellona's weapon put a hole between his eyes. At long last. She took a second to revel in the confusion on her captive's faces.

Houdini spoke up first. "I am utterly bewildered as to who you are working for."

She sighed under her breath. A shame there was so few here to hear this. Most men who needed to hear it, she had already killed.

"I work for the eleven-year-old Astro-Hungarian peasant girl who now might still have a mother and father when she is twelve. I work for all who might otherwise be crushed under the heel of the Kaiser, or the Queen, or the President, or any tyrant who thinks the world needs empires. I Bellona, work for no one—

and everyone. And as long as there are leaders like yours, I will infiltrate you and destroy you. Who knows? Next year, I may be close to your President Roosevelt. You know I can do this."

"I s'pose." Weiss spat on the deck, rising to his feet. The spit was foamy, bright red. He was hurt from the fight with Bazdt, more than he'd been letting on. "I've spent my whole life steering clear of the men you speak of." He looked at Houdini as he said this.

"You're no different, killing whoever you need to for your own plans," said Weiss. "You're as much part of the evil you claim to fight as them." He pointed at the dead Hjen lying everywhere, now in thick pools of blood.

He spat again. "Getting near the President? You could probably pull that off. But you aren't going to be around any longer than the rest of us."

The tiny suspicions nipping at her in the background of her consciousness leapt forward. She strode up to Weiss, pushing her rifle barrel up under his jaw and staring deep into his eyes. One of them had a small, orange fleck lodged in the deep blue iris.

And then it all came together. Clever, clever boy. She buried her initial panic, and saw the situation for what it was. Funny, really. She leaned in and planted a kiss fully on his lips. Why not? The first man she'd

THE BLACK CITY BENEATH

willingly kissed in twenty years and, with the life she was doomed to lead, probably the last.

She tapped the rifle barrel against his skull, hard enough to make most men wince, knowing Weiss wouldn't, purely out of pride. "You really are very good, aren't you? If all my enemies were men like you, I wouldn't need to continue. But, I must. Goodbye, Mr. Weiss. I regret that you, of all men, will likely die. But try not to."

She shoved him aside and ran for the bathysphere. As she made it through the open hatch, the last words she'd hear from Weiss rang out.

"Run! Get ready to swim!"

Chapter 23

The pressure behind Weiss' eyes mounted by the second, shooting needles of agony through the front of his skull, and Weiss wondered if the old man could take it. There were few men that could swim like the great Houdini, fewer still who knew as much about staying alive underwater, but those days had probably passed. All the time young Weiss had stood ready in the Mark V dive suit, with the escape collar that marked Houdini's first patent, he had never seen a point where Houdini needed rescuing.

That was years ago. He couldn't see him anywhere—he could barely even make out Archer just beside him through the thick brine, burning his eyes like no tomorrow. That brine was responsible for the pain his skull. Like the Dead Sea, this ocean had slowly condensed to a thick saline soup, triggered by the drying of the planet, exacerbated by the constant depletion of the Hjen's oxygen-getting methods.

Unlike the Dead Sea, this ocean seemed to harbor life, judging by the enormous creature he'd seen when the bathysphere passed through the portal. But, just as it was back on earth, the buoyancy was so high that they were positively screaming towards the surface, allowing little time for air pressure in their skulls to equalize. The result: blinding pain.

Weiss was afraid that they could easily overshoot the next launch bay further up in the city, or float past it before they could swim through the dense water towards it. But there, above, a hazy circle of lights shone through the dark murk and Weiss grabbed Archer's arm, pointing up and kicking towards it. The pain was now unbearable. And then they were through the launch bay port, bursting to the surface, gasping, desperately sucking in huge lungfuls of air.

Archer made it out of the water first, pulling himself up over the bay edge and rolling onto his back. Weiss remained for a few seconds, praying that the old man would pop up too. Then he clambered out, kneeling beside Archer in a puddle of salt water.

"Could you see him while we were swimming up?" Weiss wheezed.

"Nay. He jumped in after you, last I saw of him." Archer rolled over onto his side. "If he ain't 'ere now, I think you need fear the worst, friend."

"Well... not a man in any navy that could hold his breath as long as Harry Houdini in his prime. You

THE BLACK CITY BENEATH

wouldn't be the first to give him up for dead." Coming out of his own mouth, the words sounded like pride.

"No matter. We're all dead if we don't get away from here, far away, right now." Weiss shook away the fogginess that seemed to cloud his vision and stood up. The room spun around him and he fell back down to his knees, realizing that the ringing in his ear had changed, higher pitched and more in the background now. His balance would be shot, likely his life at sea too.

What was the sea to a dead man? They had to go *now*. Archer stood above him, reaching down and Weiss rose, taking his hand, pulling him toward a small circular sub like the one Bellona had piloted. "I watched that woman at the controls," Weiss said. "Let's see how much I learned."

Archer slapped him on the back. "I was watching too, matey."

It took less than two minutes to push the craft over the bay edge and submerge. Weiss aimed it, best guess, in the direction of the portal, descending below the Hjen City as fast as he could. From here, the vast expanse of blinking lights and spiderweb-array of shiny black tubes was even larger than he thought. It was marvel, the things these people could build. If they established a beachhead up in Washington,

207

there wasn't much doubt they would mop the floor with any army the Earth could throw at them.

"Shame you couldn't give your Dad a little more time. Must say, surprised we made it this far though."

Weiss switched his left hand to control of the yoke at the console. "Well, there's something I didn't tell you. Before you reported to the McKinely that morning, that Army engineer and I—"

The sub pitched forward violently, throwing Archer out of his seat, tossing Weiss up onto the control panel as a shrill screech—probably an alarm relating to the radical change in forward pitch—pierced the cabin. Weiss struggled to wrest the yoke from under him and right the craft, now facing down and drifting hard to starboard despite being under full power.

As he cut power and brought the nose around, working with their momentum instead of fighting it, the complex swung into view. "Good lord!" Archer shouted.

Pockets of flame, muted as quickly as they touched the water, belched from pod after pod., the lower half of the Hjen city barely visible in a roiling mass of ocean water and ejecting debris. Another bay exploded in a fire ball, tearing away the bottom half of the enormous structure. Within seconds, the lights on the upper half of the city began winking out. By the

THE BLACK CITY BENEATH

time Weiss arrested the off-course drift of the sub, the all-consuming darkness of the ocean depths had reasserted itself and the forward lights of the sub were the only illumination to be seen.

Weiss was exhausted. Otherwise, he might have smiled. "Well. In the end, that worked like a damned charm. Guess Mulholland wins the first bet. Hope he loses the second one though."

Archer was clearly in better spirits than Weiss, grinning ear-to-ear. "So you had a little surprise cooked up this whole time, you daft buggers. Can't blame you for sitting on it." He paused. "What was the second bet?"

"Whether or not we'd be court-martialed for stealing a half train-car of explosives and converting the Navy's most-advanced bathysphere into a bomb."

Any pleasure they had from successfully finding the portal and making it through was dashed when Weiss recognized the wreckage of the McKinley littering the bottom. The second bathysphere hung near the portal, but it didn't appear to be under power so they decided to take their chances in the Hjen craft. At one point, the sub lights caught a cluster of bodies, gently tumbling in a slow downward dance, and neither man spoke after that. He didn't know

R. OVERWATER

when, but at some point Weiss must have fallen asleep.

"Wake up, man!" Archer said, light penetrating the cabin; Weiss guessed they couldn't be more than a couple of fathoms down.

Small shockwaves shook the craft. Everywhere, Weiss could see bodies, wreckage, drifting bits of fabric from an airship skin, the distant outline of a gunboat, stern upwards, sinking below the surface. He also recognized, not without a small amount of pleasure, plenty of hard black material and bits of Hjen submarine, too. However tough that stuff was, apparently a 14-inch shell could break it.

Archer was clearly excited. "Somebody's givin' somebody hell up there!"

The cabin brightened, signaling that they were about to hit the surface: "We're piloting an enemy ship!" Weiss said. He jammed the yoke forward and fumbled for the sub's throttle but they were already up and above.

The overcast sky was mottled with thick gouts of smoke. Warships, spread as far as the eye could see, peppered the air with heavy gunfire and through the canopy they heard the unceasing thunderous rumble of steady cannon fire. To their port side, a Prussian airship drifted sideways. Fire consumed its aft end as tiny figures leaped from the gondola into the choppy

210

THE BLACK CITY BENEATH

sea and slipped below the waves. Weiss squinted at the bow of the closest ship. The *Storozhevoy*: a ship he knew for a fact had been stationed in Alaska.

Of course. Since it was truly the Prussians behind all the double-dealing and death, Russia would have easily become allies in the battle. Hopefully that had tipped the odds—there was no way to tell who was winning down here in the water.

"We need to get out of this damn thing! Archer pointed to a Virginia-class gunboat coming into view. Weiss made out a figure with binoculars feverishly pointing in their direction, two sailors beside him swinging a small deck gun around towards the Hjen sub. They were still aiming as a round from somewhere else rocked the sub and the front port quarter of the sub exploded in a cloud of shrapnel, lacerating his face and blowing Weiss through the shattered canopy into the water.

Down was barely discernible from up, waves splashing over him in rapid succession, stinging in what felt like a thousand cuts. When he got his face to the surface for a breath, blood streamed down into his eyes, obscuring all vision, and his nose and throat burned from the smell of the explosive shell, both ears ringing from the detonation. He could feel his own weight pulling him down beneath the water. Weiss

211

R. OVERWATER

knew: if he went more than a couple feet under, even for a second, he wasn't coming back up.

Part of the Hjen sub was still floating. He reached desperately, only to be blown back again as another round struck it. Kicking with everything he had, he forced his head above the surface again. He could see something still floating, maybe he could reach it. A wave pushed him forward to it, rolling over him mid breath and choking him with a lungful of saltwater. When he could see again, his heart sank.

It was Archer, face down, arms and legs slack and spread wide. Weiss could see a large Opace shard from sub's hull protruding from his back, and the crimson pool spreading around him left no doubt as to the divemaster's fate. Weiss tried calling out his name, producing only a weak cough. Then, somewhere, there was another explosion. Something deep below.

A thump went right through his body. Before him, a gigantic swell rose, tall as a building, massive and circular, spreading in a circle. Ships bobbed and tossed, a couple capsizing. The wave lifted him up as it crested. A deep void where the wave had been centered opened in a rush of wind, followed by a colossal sucking sound. A small destroyer cartwheeled into it, looking like a toy as it fell. Water folded over it, as if it had never been.

THE BLACK CITY BENEATH

Something struck Weiss from behind and he lost consciousness.

Chapter 24

Voices. Somewhere in a dark velvet murk, there were voices. "*Eto Amerikanskiy moryak!*" A dim glimpse of black and white-striped arms reaching out. Darkness again.

And then eyes. A woman's eyes, deep and clear, boring into his own, piercing right through him. Fear, distrust, an icy hand gripping his heart. But something, deeper within those eyes, clear, true and honest too. Something that belied an evil facade, confusing what was real and what wasn't. The confusion swelled and Weiss floated in something dark like the sea—but that was not the sea—images rippling past him as the confusion solidified into doubt and displacement. The face of his father, the helmet lowering over his eyes, the sight of a dirigible fragmenting across an ocean surface, dead sailors in countless sunken ships, the deadly line of a rifle barrel, toppling figures of unmistakable malevolence.

Light, all-consuming white, crowded the edges of the darkness, a creeping circle spreading inwards to

R. OVERWATER

the centre. Weiss could feel the surface coming closer and he fought to swim back down, deep where danger was far away, where a man could be alone.

But still the eyes stayed, the message lodged far in the back of them becoming clearer. Confusion turned to realization and dismay. The hiding place was gone, forever unreachable now, and there was no choice but to be counted among those that made decisions, terrible ones perhaps, and live with them. And then the light turned to colors, yellows, oranges, warmth—sunlight, through a window. He was above the surface now, just the fleeting images of the eyes, and as the realization struck that he was alive and in a room, a name attached to those eyes. The name of a dead woman.

"Bellona," Weiss croaked feebly.

"Eh?" Melville leaned forward in his chair. He stared intently at Weiss, inches from his face. Melville's image became clearer. Around Weiss, a hospital room drifted into focus. Behind Melville, Mulholland sat with one arm in a sling.

"Mulholland!" said Melville. "After all these weeks, the lad is finally back among the living!"

Mulholland's face came into view. "Whaddaya know?" the engineer said. "When they put you in that decompression chamber, I began to worry you weren't impossible to kill after all. Here. Take a swig of water."

216

THE BLACK CITY BENEATH

A steel claw swung into sight, Mulholland reaching into his suit coat and fiddling with something on his chest. The claw released, depositing the glass on the bedside table.

He looked taken aback, reading the expression Weiss must have had on his face. One of Mulholland's eyes was covered by gauze. One shoulder drooped from the weight of what was most certainly not a real arm. "I sure got some stories for you, pal. And made a few improvements while you slept." He shook the shoulder with the metal arm in its sleeve, and pointed to a sketchpad over on the windowsill. "Don't worry, I'll have one custom built to hold a rod and reel by the time you get us to Cuba."

Weiss would have laughed, if he could have. Instead, realizing how muffled everything was, he lifted his head off the pillow. Things immediately sounded crisp again, and he remembered—one ear was likely shot for good now. "So how did we do?" he asked.

"The Prussian advance was halted, thanks to the Russians and Mr. Mulholland here," said Melville. "He kept power going long enough to trigger his device. Luckily, you had just popped through."

"The Hjen submarine fleet—"

Mulholland grinned. "It occurred to me that the stuff we were playing with might have the strength to

217

unbalance the whole portal if we directed all our power at it. I decided not to wait for clearance. A couple scouts got through, but it looks like we all but closed the thing up before the next wave. Luckily, it looks like they were holding back until the Prussians softened us up." Mulholland looked smug. "They missed their chance."

"Indeed," Melville chimed in. "Her Majesty's Engineering Corp has requested him as guest of honor at their annual awards."

"But first," Mulholland was all smiles now, "Roosevelt's bringing us back to Washington to pin some medals on us. You can bet, I'm buying fares for the whole family to come see that."

Mulholland leaned in and whispered, "Did you use our little surprise?" Weiss nodded and Mulholland slapped his leg. "Yes!"

Weiss felt sleep coming on. Not unconsciousness, but genuine, restful sleep.

Weiss felt silly using the cane to board the train to New York. The doctors assured him his balance would come back enough to discard it eventually, although he might never truly get his sea legs back. A knock on the door of his berth came before he could settle in and he slid the panel open. It was Major Bertha Tharpe, with a small brown paper-wrapped

THE BLACK CITY BENEATH

parcel in her arms. Two Army privates stood behind here, each holding one end of a steamer trunk.

"Glad we caught you in time." The wrinkles round her eyes crinkled further, almost mischievously. "To be honest, when they named you as the sea rat to help my top man, I objected. I've never been so wrong in my life."

She pushed the package into his hands and pointed to an empty corner. The privates dropped the trunk there and beelined out. "The Russians sent you this, and the contents of the trunk too. I guess they found some of your personal gear on the beach."

Weiss looked at the package. The writing on it was in Russian.

"Good-bye, Master Diver Weiss. It's been a pleasure." Tharpe turned and exited and Weiss gratefully closed the door, collapsing on the cushioned bench. As the train lurched into motion, he resumed his thoughts. Melville and Wilkie were crestfallen when Weiss relayed the story of his last moments with Harry Houdini. No man could fill his shoes, they said, and he was needed more than ever. But Weiss knew who else could do it. If he had to.

He had to. Despite their triumphs, a war that would sweep across the world was still coming. He could feel it. It was time, as his father had, as Bellona, Mulholland, and so many others had, to

219

muster a sense of conscience and best determine what was right—pick a direction, a side, and fight for it. The Houdini Manufacturing Company had played a part in that, and could again.

In New York, there would be Houdini's secret office safe. When the great magician prompted him for the combination after administering the helmet treatment, it had been a red herring, the first sign his father was up to more than he was letting on. There was no combination at all; only a man with Houdini's knowledge of locking mechanisms would ever crack it and open it. In it, most likely, there would be a will bequeathing everything to Weiss—who had always kept the immigrant family's last name, despite his father changing his for show business purposes. There would likely be a deposition explaining how and why Houdini had so carefully hidden his only child. He was too much of a planner to have not thought that far ahead.

Exactly what Weiss would do after that, he didn't know. The government would likely have no shortage of suggestions. He fingered the parcel, finally peeling back the brown paper. It was a small box, containing only a note. The handwriting was Harry Houdini's.

"My only son. Who I obviously trained better than he might ever admit to a less than warm father: I'm sorry for everything. And now, the insurmountable

THE BLACK CITY BENEATH

evidence that could cause people with the best intentions to publicly hang for their perceived crimes has created familiar bedfellows. Do not seek us, we dare not let ourselves be found. Just know that our crimes saved thousands of lives for every one they cost. I will not in good conscience actually follow Bellona's path, of course. But be aware that she is out there somewhere."

Weiss turned the paper over, finding more on the back. "Bellona says what is left of the Hjen City still contains secrets that must never fall into the wrong hands. There is a special key to her hiding places, she says you will know it when you see it. Always do right, son. I say this fully believing you are incapable of anything but."

He folded the note. He was not shocked the man had survived. But she was alive too. And how did he feel about that? He couldn't explain her survival. Had she found the bomb, but left it ticking nonetheless? He stood, unfastened the trunk lid, and looked inside.

It was his original Mark V dive suit, the suit he'd worn all those hours at the escape artist's side underwater. Old habits kicked in and he pulled the haphazardly packed contents out, laying them on the floor and going through the pieces one by one, squaring them away for future sea duty. A sleeve was

221

R. OVERWATER

torn, but it was otherwise ship-shape. In the helmet, he found strands of dark-black hair.

And in one leaden boot, he found a gold necklace with a black Opace pearl pendant. He remembered it instantly. The last time he'd seen it, the gold circled an elegant, tanned neck under opulent lighting, the black pendant lying against smooth skin wrapped in green velvet.

Epilogue

Bellona cursed the Kentucky hayseed most of all. She had barely made it into the Supreme's secret bunker when the floor rippled, like a wave passing across water, and the room shook with the sound of rending metal. Panicked screams, barely muted by the reinforced walls, were drowned out as klaxons sounded. The door seal flexed and water wept around the edges. The moisture began to bubble like a spring and in seconds became a thin, high-pressure spray. If she drowned here, it would be Mulholland's doing.

It had taken her several minutes to find the bomb's switch tucked under a bench in the American vessel. A push button, designed to close a circuit that could only be broken once she got under the deck plating they'd welded over top of it. It took several more minutes to find a Hjen pistol and bang on the decking, sounding out a safe hollow spot where she could blast a hole through and hopefully avoid detonating the bomb.

R. OVERWATER

Once she had wormed through the hole, the dim light revealed the extent of Mulholland's cunning. It was a simple bomb, requiring a basic circuit, a battery and a clock; one that currently showed only a few minutes remaining. But the American engineer had spliced numerous wires in, disguising which were positive, which were negative, which were ground wires, and which ones would actually detonate all of the trinitrotoluene.

TNT was a newer explosive, one she was an unabashed proponent of, but she cursed Mulholland's ingenuity nonetheless. They'd obviously set the clock with enough time for Weiss to have a chance of escaping. He'd cut it close, but he'd probably made it out of the Black City. Bellona undoubtedly could have determined a safe way to dismantle the bomb but she, unlike Weiss, only had three minutes. She'd given up and run for the bunker. This bay was closest to the command center; she'd made it. But now what?

If only she'd had time to look for a dive suit. She pulled an emergency breather, good for a few minutes, out of the bunker's supply locker and slipped the mouthpiece between her teeth. Gripping the door release firmly, she twisted and allowed the water pressure to sweep the door back and pin her against the wall, protecting her from the barrage of flotsam.

THE BLACK CITY BENEATH

The water was frigid and pain stabbed through her skull as she swam out. An emergency light shone dimly ahead and she saw the entire bay hanging like a nearly severed limb on a bundle of twisted piping. Bodies floated everywhere. One of them was the Supreme. *Burial at sea. More than you deserve*, she thought.

Any usable escape craft was either destroyed or had fallen to the sea floor. She needed a Hjen dive suit. There had to be one somewhere, but she could barely see in the submerged gloom. She kicked hard and the ruptured husk of the bathysphere appeared, lying against the down-most wall of the suspended bay structure.

Something slapped against her face, covering her eyes. She pulled it back; a canvas sleeve with a rubber mitt. A piece of one of the Americans' primitive suits. She swam to the bathysphere. Fortunately the bomb's blast had sought an avenue through the thinner hull bottom instead of the thick interior deck plating they'd welded over top of it. Parts of the bathysphere were still intact.

Off to one side, she saw another U.S. suit, an older one with a metal waist collar. Bellona had done her research; she knew what had launched Harry Houdini's manufacturing company. His son had brought this down. In a rack near the suit was an

225

emergency waist tank. The man they'd sent to destroy her might have just saved her.

After climbing into the suit, holding her breath until she could open the emergency tank, she tucked the all-but-depleted emergency breather under her arm—just in case. Cautiously, she worked her way to the edge of the ruptured bay, hanging on tightly.

The structure could break loose at any time and send her careening to the seabed. The suit was clumsy, too large for her frame, the boots and gloves flopping at the end of her limbs, and the brass helmet was too heavy to swim with. She was trapped.

A light flickered in the distance. It grew closer. An escape sub, adrift, but the lights inside were on. A figure was inside, trying to right himself as the craft slowly barrel-rolled. Harry Houdini.

Bombs were crude devices, an unavoidable necessity sometimes, and Bellona had gotten her fill of them lately. The same with devices like the one Mulholland set off just after they were clear of the portal. Walking across the stone courtyard of Hohenzollern Castle, the disgust was overwhelming though. The whole edifice needed to come down, and a bomb would do it. But to kill the Kaiser, holed up and more paranoid than ever, she would need to be at his side and make sure the job was complete.

THE BLACK CITY BENEATH

He was undoubtedly surprised that she had reported in after the failure of the invasion, on the eve of an inevitable retaliation. Perhaps the Kaiser would order her executed after their meeting. No matter, she'd be executed after she shot him anyway. There was virtually no way of escaping all the way down the mountainside, let alone through the narrow, guarded hallways of the castle. She wouldn't even have the quietness of a Hjen pistol on her side when it was time.

The Prussian winter air was cold, but the sky was clear and frost crystals on the trees glittered like jewels in the sunlight. After breathing the Hjen's stink for so long, the crisp air smelled like purity itself. A cadre of young *Schattenpistolen*, some no doubt stolen from their lives as she had been, saluted as she passed by them. It was a fine day to kill the last man on her list.

Perhaps the winter weather was similarly splendid in New York. Harry Houdini had guessed that was where his son would go. Karl Weiss—what would he do next? Bellona entertained herself with the idea that she might go observe him. Not contact him of course, just watch him for a little while and be sure he was up to something she could approve of. Her work might take her in that direction anyways.

227

She hadn't decided if President Roosevelt would be the start of a new list or not.

When she arrived at the Kaiser's meeting room, he had yet to be ushered in. She could tell by the way the guards alternated between staring at each other and their own boots on the burnished marble floor, and the manner in which they nervously touched their weapons, that a trap had been laid. Indeed, one had.

They probably wouldn't shoot her on the spot, opting instead for a trial, followed by a firing squad. The Supreme, Grunvald, Bazdt, they had got what they deserved, the same as the Kaiser would get. Cold-hearted killers that made the world a more terrible place than it should be. She was a killer too so, fine, she would be executed. Wasn't that the one thing Bellona had desired since she was twelve? A world where killers got what they deserved?

She looked out the window, estimating the distance between its ledge and the balcony below. Yes, yes, they all deserved to die. And her as well. But she didn't have to make it easy for them.

Mentions

A big thank you to those who gave me a second wind, and the places that gave me a second home to write in.

Geoff Cole, Axel Howerton, Robert Bose, Sarah L. Johnson, Hayden Trenholm, Renee Bennett, Greg Chomichuk, Robert Vardeman, Kevin Weir, The Ship and Anchor, The Wild Rose Taproom, Bobby's Old World Tavern.

About the Author

Rick Overwater is a Calgary-based journalist, fiction author, and nationally distributed recording artist/songwriter. His latest graphic novel, *Futility: Orange Planet Horror* was shortlisted for the Canadian Science Fiction and Fantasy Association's 2019 Aurora Award in the graphic novel category. His latest short story, "House of the Knight's Nail," appears in the anthology By the Light of Camelot, also nominated for a 2019 Aurora. Several of his crime stories and speculative fiction are available in a number of anthologies, his nonfiction has appeared in publications ranging from Snowboard Canada to the Globe and Mail, and his songs have made it onto Canadian campus-radio top-ten charts.

Rick is midway through his Master's Degree in Creative Writing at the University of British Columbia and tries to make time for craft beer, his guitar collection, and sometimes even his wife and two children. He can be found at www.overwater.ca, on Facebook under Rick Overwater, on Twitter at @rjoverwater and on Instagram at rjoverwater.

Visit us online at
www.the-seventh-terrace.com/tiny-sledgehammer

CPSIA information can be obtained
at www.ICGtesting.com
Printed in the USA
BVHW070946010223
657353BV00001B/11